TANGLED BREATHS OF LOVE

A FICTION INSPIRED BY TRUE EVENTS

SMRITI GUPTA

Made with ♥ on the Notion Press Platform
www.notionpress.com

Dedicated to you

Within these pages, may you discover whispers of your own narrative

— a symphony of hopes, dreams, and boundless potential.

For in love, every soul discovers life's true essence.

Contents

Contents

Disclaimer

This book is a work of fiction. While certain elements of the storyline may be inspired by real events, the characters, incidents, dialogues, organizations, and settings in this novel are products of the author's imagination. Any resemblance to actual persons, living or dead, or real events is purely coincidental. The author has taken creative liberties to craft a unique and original story based on themes drawn from various experiences. The content within is intended for mature audiences and contains themes and situations suitable for adult readers. Reader discretion is advised.

Acknowledgements

In the symphony of my life's narrative, countless melodies harmonize, each note resonating with the love, support, and unwavering faith of those who shaped my story.

To my cherished life partner, whose unwavering belief in my dreams has been a steadfast anchor in every storm and a beacon of unwavering support in every triumph. Amidst the whirlwind of emotions that at times swept us both away, you stood resolute, a rock in the tumultuous currents. Like a lighthouse guiding a weary traveller, your patience illuminated our path through serene and chaotic moments. Your love, an intricate thread woven delicately into the fabric of our shared journey, has adorned these pages with an unparalleled depth of emotion and resilience. For your enduring presence amidst the whirlwind of emotions, I am eternally grateful.

To my incredible parents, whose boundless sacrifices and enduring encouragement planted the seeds of ambition and resilience within me. Your guidance forms the bedrock upon which my aspirations stand tall. Your wisdom and unwavering support have instilled in me a foundation of values, morals, and determination, upon which I build my dreams and pursuits. Your sacrifices, often unnoticed yet profoundly felt, have been the fertile soil in which my potential took root. The depths of your love and sacrifices resonate in every word penned within these pages, a testament to the profound impact you have had on the person I have become.

To my dear brother, a constant companion in the labyrinth of life's adventures. Our shared escapades, whether woven with mischief or cloaked in profound conversations, have shaped the chapters of my story. Your camaraderie and shared laughter have painted the brightest hues on the canvas of my memories.

Through thick and thin, you have been a beacon of unwavering support, and your presence continues to colour the narratives of my life with a richness that makes every memory a treasure.

To my extended family, a mosaic of love and diverse perspectives, each one contributing a unique brushstroke to the masterpiece of my existence. Your collective presence has made my journey richer and more vibrant.

And to the divine force that guides us all, an omnipresent source of strength and solace. In moments of doubt, your silent guidance has illuminated the path forward, infusing these pages with a spiritual resonance that transcends the ordinary.

To all those who unwaveringly believed in me and to those who doubted my abilities, your contrasting beliefs have fueled my determination and shaped my journey in profound ways. Thank you for being part of my story.

Your collective influence, love, and presence have crafted not just this book, but the very essence of who I am. With deepest gratitude, I humbly acknowledge your immeasurable impact on my life's tapestry.

Prologue

Lying on the cold, hard ground, his face began to blur as my consciousness waned. I was on the brink of losing consciousness.

A metallic taste lingered on my lips, mixing with the salty drops falling upon them. Amid the haze, his face appeared, his voice crying out my name in despair, “Sayami, please stay with me. Don’t close your eyes."

The constant voice was slipping into the abyss of my soul, its echoes growing fainter with each heavy blink in the dim stadium light. His cold hands, stained crimson, clutched me tightly. I could feel the searing pain spreading from my chest. I knew I was bleeding.

The stadium lights cast an eerie glow, illuminating the green grass, a stark contrast to the encroaching darkness. My gaze, fading from his face to the starlit sky, found solace in the moon’s familiar glow. Metaphorically, he was my moon – appearing close yet inexplicably distant. Just like the moon’s eternal presence, I knew he would always be there, seemingly within reach. But, like the enigmatic satellite, he remained emotionally distant, hovering just out of grasp. As I lay there once more, with him standing above me, I realized our paths would never converge, at least not in this lifetime. That is why he was my moon.

The cold breeze scourged my deep wound but the sound of the man I loved was balmy. I was always afraid of losing someone who could never be mine but in this very moment, I felt free.

He cradled my head, fingers entwined in my hair, holding onto the remnants of my existence. His once triumphant arms, now a source of solace, attempted to preserve the last vestiges of my life. The distant roars of the crowd, now an echo from another world, felt disconnected from the intimate tragedy unfolding on the field. My breaths came in shallow gasps, growing weaker with each passing moment. The air itself felt depleted of vitality. He brushed my hair gently, his touch tender, his eyes filled with a mix of love and helplessness. The scent of grass mingled with salt, evoking a bittersweet aroma that encapsulated the moment of loss and despair. My head rested upon his chest, and amidst my fading senses, I discerned a different rhythm in his heartbeat. His heart was beating for me, a tune once my cherished melody. But now, it posed a haunting question – how could he hurt a heart that loved him so deeply?

In the final moments, the football field transformed into a sacred ground for an inevitable farewell. The expansive green expanse, witness to countless victories, now bore witness to a love transcending the boundaries of life and death. As I closed my eyes one last time, he held me close, tears merging with the dew on the grass, grieving not only my life but also the unspoken dreams we shared on this hallowed ground.

I was dying but a part of me was happy within. As the darkness closed in, I found a strange comfort in the fact that at least at this moment, he held me close, his emotions undeniably sincere. In his presence, an ever-present uncertainty loomed large, an unpredictable dichotomy between being wounded or enveloped in love with each passing moment. Since his arrival, life had been a relentless storm of struggles and heartaches. Still, an unrelenting affection kept pulling me back to him, yearning for stolen moments of joy and fleeting displays of tenderness.

In this final embrace, his arms wrapped around me and quenched a long-felt longing. Through his eyes, I glimpsed the depth of his affection, the remorse for unspoken confessions, and the anguish of our shared, unacknowledged love story. A love that never found its voice, never danced upon his lips, yet reverberated through every touch, every lingering gaze, and every tender moment we shared.

As my fading gaze traced the contours of his face, I found myself marvelling at the beauty of our unspoken connection. Words, I realized, were not always necessary to convey the most profound of emotions. In his arms, I discovered a love that transcended language, speaking in the silent eloquence of gestures, glances, and countless unspoken promises.

Under the cloak of starry nights, I frequently delved into the labyrinth of my musings, pondering our journey. I often wondered why he refrained from voicing the sentiments that his eyes eloquently conveyed. His gaze contained myriad emotions, akin to entire galaxies, yet the verbal declaration of love remained unspoken. His stolen glances lingered on me, reminiscent of a poet captivated by love, yet an expansive silence enveloped us, mirroring the vastness of the night sky above.

I wished he had summoned the courage to voice his heart, to let love flow freely like a river finding its course. But as I drew my final breath, I found solace in the knowledge that our unspoken love was real. It formed the backdrop of our shared moments, the silent melody underscoring our story.

In the recesses of my heart, I questioned if he feared the vulnerability that love demanded. Or perhaps, he believed his actions spoke louder than words, a story of love conveyed through gestures and kindness. I wondered if past heartaches scarred him, making him wary of expressing his affections. Did he doubt if I would fathom the depths of his emotions? Did he deem his love inadequate despite every touch, smile, and shared moment narrating a different tale?

Amidst my introspection, I also considered if he had not fully comprehended the depths of his feelings "Love is indeed a labyrinth of emotions, and perhaps he found himself entangled within its intricate complexities, uncertain of how to articulate or unravel its depths.

So, amid my wondering, I chose to revel in the unspoken language that passed between us. His love, though silent, was a tangible presence, a warmth that wrapped around my soul. In his touch, his glances, and his actions, I found a love so profound that it surpassed the need for words. And in that, I discovered a truth - love, in all its forms, was boundless, whether expressed in poetry or written in the silent eloquence of a gaze.

In the quiet of that final embrace, I sent him a silent message of love, a whispered reassurance that I understood, that I felt his affection even in the silence. And with a fleeting smile, I let go, not of love unreturned, but of a love that had enriched my life in ways words could never capture.

As I closed my eyes for the last time, I carried with me the memory of his touch, the echo of his unspoken love, and the serenity of knowing that in his arms, I had experienced a love that, though never verbalized, had been the most profound and beautiful chapter of my life.

His eyes crying out in fear of losing someone he kept pushing at an insurmountable space. This time, I did not despair, pleading for him to thaw the icy walls surrounding his distant heart. Instead, I was letting him go, bidding adieu to the fragments of our intertwined lives and our story destined to never reach the culmination of a happy circle.

1

New Beginnings

As the day to leave for college approached, my room, once a sanctuary, felt both comforting and suffocating. The idea of stepping into a world filled with strangers was overwhelming for someone like me – an introvert who found solace in the familiar corners of her room and the quietude of her own thoughts.

The anticipation of leaving the cocoon of my home ignited a whirlwind of conflicting emotions. On one hand, there was an eagerness to learn, to explore the subjects I loved, and to embrace the intellectual challenges that college promised. On the other hand, the prospect of social interactions, crowded lecture halls, and dormitory life seemed like a storm I was ill-prepared to weather. While my heart fluttered with excitement for this new chapter, the quiet introvert in me could not help but feel the weight of homesickness bearing down on me.

The thought of making friends, engaging in small talk, and navigating the complexities of social circles made my heart race with anxiety. The very idea of orientation events and dormitory gatherings sent shivers down my spine. I questioned my ability to fit in, to find my place amidst the extroverted laughter and lively conversations that echoed through the college brochures.

College, with its enticing promises of forging new friendships and embarking on thrilling adventures, presented a world vastly different from the tranquil haven of solitude I had grown accustomed to. As someone who had always been emotionally sensitive, even the smallest things left profound imprints on my heart.

The notion of vibrant dormitories, clamorous dining halls, and ceaseless social engagements stirred waves of anxiety within my typically composed demeanor. The thought of leaving behind the comforting embrace of my family, my quiet reading nook, and the peaceful walks through my neighbourhood felt like saying goodbye to a part of myself.

I cherished the thought of learning and growing, but the introvert in me craved the tranquillity of my own space, the solace of a good book, and the serenity of self-reflection. The prospect of navigating a sea of unfamiliar faces and engaging in small talk left me feeling vulnerable, like a fragile bird leaving its nest for the first time.

But amidst the trepidation, there was a glimmer of hope. I knew that this journey was a necessary step towards independence and personal growth. I had always yearned for a deeper connection with the world beyond my comfort zone, even if it meant stepping out of it.

The night before departure, I sat by my window, gazing at the moon in the starlit sky, seeking solace in the silent brilliance. My mind raced with questions – Would I find friends who understood my need for solitude? Would I be able to balance the demands of social interactions with my introverted nature? The unknowns stretched out before me like an endless, intimidating abyss.

As I closed my eyes that night, I made a silent promise to myself – to embrace the discomfort, to step out of my comfort zone, but also to honour my introverted nature. I acknowledged that it was okay to seek solitude, to recharge in the quiet moments, and to let my thoughts breathe.

The next morning, as I hugged my family goodbye, I carried with me the wisdom of introversion. I knew that it was okay to seek solitude when I needed it, to recharge in the quiet moments, and to find solace in the simple joys that life offered. I also knew that I could gradually build connections with like-minded souls who understood the beauty of introversion.

With a deep breath and a heart full of both fear and determination, I stepped into the unknown fully aware that the homesickness would come and go like waves. College was a new chapter, a daunting one, but it was an opportunity to learn, to grow, and to live my new beginnings in my own quiet, introverted way.

2

Ruthless Assembly

Here I stood, facing the gates of a whole new world—the esteemed Renaissance School of Sciences. The sight before me was a congregation of young faces, each a part of a different clique—laughter, fervor, and geekiness abound. Every individual seemed wrapped in the restless energy of a Nuckelavee, making me jittery as I grappled with the baggage I carried, uncertain about whom to approach for directions.

Stepping onto the bustling college campus, a wave of emotions surged within me—a blend of excitement and apprehension. The air buzzed with the promise of fresh beginnings, yet my heart, aching with homesickness, carried the weight of farewells and unfamiliarity.

I had secured a full scholarship to RSS, a testament to my hard work and dedication. Nestled in the heart of a city adorned with skyscrapers, my family lived, not amongst riches, but among humble, hardworking folks. My parents, resilient and industrious, laboured away in blue-collar jobs. My father, his weathered hands testament to years of toil, worked tirelessly as a handyman. Meanwhile, my mother, with her unwavering smile and unwavering spirit, served as a compassionate caregiver for the elderly.

Their tireless efforts imparted in me the conviction that education held the key to a brighter future. With limited resources, I had to put in twice the effort, burning the midnight oil while juggling multiple responsibilities to keep my aspirations afloat. Each day melted into the next, and I immersed myself in learning, absorbing knowledge like a parched land soaking up rain. I became not just a scholar, but a seeker of wisdom—driven by passion and resolute in my pursuit of success.

The scholarship was not merely a piece of paper; it was a lifeline, a golden ticket to a future that had seemed out of reach. When the news arrived, tears of joy and relief cascaded down my cheeks. It signified the fulfilment of not just my dreams but those of my parents too.

In my teenage years, my experiences were mostly confined to late-night library sessions and the company of Taani. She was charismatic and stylish, effortlessly capturing attention wherever she went—my only friend and pillar of support. Socializing for me was limited to our joint birthday celebrations, marked by my mother's delicious pineapple cake, a token we shared each evening. Over the years, Taani became my confidante, problem-solver, attentive listener, and my source of humour during life's highs and lows.

Taani, a social butterfly, effortlessly mingled with her circle of friends whenever she was not with me. Yet, I remained her closest confidante. I helped her with calculus and thermodynamics, while she guided me in choosing the perfect shade of lipstick to complement my outfits—although, truth be told, I hardly ever wore any makeup.

Growing up together, we shared study sessions, squabbles, weekend movie marathons of old Disney classics, and adventurous hikes through the woods, be it in rain, snow, or sunshine. We would dash into the woods across the road, laughing uproariously as we tumbled in the snow, creating beautiful snow angels.

Now, as Taani flew to a college abroad, I found myself alone, with dreams of a future in science. Despite our separation, we vowed to keep our bond strong, promising to remain in touch, sharing tales of our melancholy over being apart—especially mine.

As the sun descended below the horizon, elongating the shadows across the unfamiliar campus, I stood at a crossroads, my mind swirling with thoughts. Clutching the straps of my bags, I scanned the array of buildings, the buzz of excited student chatter filling the air. Despite the lively surroundings, uncertainty fluttered in my heart. Navigating the maze-like corridors of the administration building, I finally encountered a sign pointing me toward the "male and female dorms." Relief washed over me, and I hastened my steps toward the female dormitory.

In the heart of the college campus, just before the entrance, an unusual energy crackled in the air. Excitement mingled with tension and youthful confidence. A crowd of students gathered, drawn in like moths to a flame, as two figures engaged in a heated argument. Suddenly, a punch was thrown, swift and forceful, igniting a chain reaction of violence. Cheers erupted, a chaotic symphony of encouragement and adrenaline, fueling the combatants.

Fists darted through the air like lightning bolts, the impact muffled by the growing roar of voices. It was a raw clash, propelled by ego, pride, and perhaps the influence of alcohol. Amidst the chaos, friends exchanged celebratory gestures, strangers bonded over shared enthusiasm, and the spirit of unity intertwined with the cheering students. The scene unfolded in a surreal fashion, blending youthful exuberance with the primal rush of competition.

Security guards rushed in, their uniforms a stark contrast against the chaos. Their attempts to restore order were met with resistance, the combatants too engrossed in their battle to heed the calls for peace. It took a collective effort, a joint plea from friends and bystanders, to finally quell the storm.

Keeping a straight and low face, I dared not even see the ruthless assembly; I continued walking towards the dorm. But with the peripheral vision and cramped spaces between the bodies hovering in the crowd, I saw two faces- the face of a brutally beaten guy, lying there, bleeding his mouth and nose, abundant black-blue bruises, and swollen eyes, and the other guy who held him in his clutch and was still landing ruthless punches to what seemed like a half-dead victim.

I was petrified, my breath quickened, matching the pace of my hurried steps as I moved away as swiftly as my legs would allow. I could hardly regain my senses until I banged against someone, losing my balance, and falling on my face. I looked up and saw a girl lending her hand for me to stand up.

With black curly hair framing her face and glasses perched on her nose, she turned to me and inquired, "Are you a freshman?"

Her question caught me off guard, and I instinctively reached out, taking her hand for support. After a moment to collect myself, I replied tentatively, unsure if I had made a blunder on my very first day. "Um, yes. I... I am a freshman. My name is Sayami," I stammered.

A smile played on her lips, and I could not help but wonder if she found my nervousness amusing.

"I'm Eila. And I am a second-year student," she introduced herself.

Setting my bags down, we exchanged smiles.

After a brief pause, I gathered the courage to ask, "Could you please direct me to room number 10B?"

"Room 10B is on the first floor. I will take you there. Mine is 12B. Looks like you will be my neighbor," she exclaimed, her voice filled with enthusiasm.

Her joy was palpable, as if she had found a long-lost friend. While I usually took a considerable amount of time to get close to someone, her warmth was unexpectedly comforting, making this connection a welcomed surprise.

Taking one of my bags, she guided me toward my room. Despite the old saying that "seniors aren't friends of freshmen," her demeanour remained cheerful and amiable.

As I cautiously opened the door to my dormitory room, she settled in comfortably while I began unpacking and arranging my belongings.

The space was a blank canvas, waiting to be painted with memories and personal touches. The room, though compact, held the promise of independence and growth. With each step, the creak of the floorboards echoed the anticipation in my heart. I took a deep breath, inhaling the scent of new beginnings, as I surveyed the room. The sunlight filtered through the curtains, casting a warm, golden glow over the bare walls.

I started by unpacking my belongings, each item a piece of my identity. My favourite books found a home on the shelf, their familiar spines a source of comfort. Posters of inspiring quotes and artwork adorned the walls, transforming the space into a sanctuary of motivation and creativity.

As I unfolded my bedsheets, I imagined the nights of studying and laughter that would soon fill this room. The soft duvet, in hues of calming blues, promised nights of peaceful sleep after long days of learning.

The desk became my command centre, where textbooks and notebooks found their place alongside a cluster of pens and a potted plant, adding a touch of nature to the room. A string of fairy lights hung delicately, casting a soft, ethereal glow in the evenings, illuminating my late-night study sessions.

In one corner, I set up a cosy reading nook, complete with a plush chair and a floor lamp. This was where I planned to escape into the world of literature, finding solace and adventure between the pages of my favourite novels. The room gradually transformed into a reflection of my personality and aspirations. It became more than just a space; it became my haven, a cocoon where I would evolve, learn, and create lasting friendships. As I stood back to admire my work, I felt a sense of pride and anticipation.

The dormitory room represented more than mere physical space; it stood as a symbol of my transition into adulthood. It was a testament to my resilience, a place where I aimed to adapt, grow, and, perhaps, shed some of my introverted tendencies. With a heart full of hope and excitement, I felt ready to embrace the adventures that awaited me in this newfound home away from home.

However, another moment, amidst the well-set belongings and the posters, I put up to make it feel like home, a profound sense of homesickness settled in. The room, once so alien, now seemed like a sanctuary, but it was not enough to fill the void left by the comforting familiarity of my bedroom. I found myself longing for the sound of my mom's voice, the smell of my dad's cooking, and the soft purring of my cat. Every laugh in the hallway, every clinking of plates in the cafeteria, reminded me of the family dinners and inside jokes I had left behind.

Eila interrupted my thoughts with a knowing smile and began explaining the intricacies of college life, becoming a beacon of guidance amidst the sea of new experiences. She could tell me every possible thing about the college.

"First things first, remember your schedule is your best friend. Make sure to jot down your classes, the timings, and the locations. Trust me, it will save you from running around like a headless chicken," she said, her tone laced with a touch of humour.

"As for professors, each one has their unique teaching style. Some are strict, some are lenient. But they all appreciate students who are attentive and engaged. Do not hesitate to ask questions if you are confused. Professors love students who show genuine interest in their subjects," the senior advised, her eyes twinkling with wisdom earned from experience.

"And oh, the library! It is not just a quiet place to study; it is a treasure trove of knowledge. Make friends with the librarians; they can be your best allies during research projects. Speaking of friends, do not hesitate to reach out. College is not just about academics; it is also about the connections you make. Attend club meetings, join societies, and participate in events. You will find people who share your interests," she continued, her enthusiasm infectious.

"And about the campus itself, explore every nook and cranny. Each corner holds a story, a memory waiting to be made. And do not forget about the cafeteria; it is not just a place for food but also socializing. Many great friendships begin over a cup of coffee or a plate of fries," the senior added, her smile widening.

From navigating the dynamics of senior-junior interactions to encountering both the coolest and the grumpiest professors, the whirlwind of college festivals, and mingling with celebrity students alongside the looming specter of exams and grades at RSS. She was a relentless chatterbox. I, on the other hand, played the role of the attentive listener, rarely interrupting her lively narratives—until she turned the conversation around, prompting me to share more about myself.

“I am an introvert, so I find my energy in the quiet moments, often lost in the pages of a good book or immersed in my studies. My world revolves around the written word, and I believe that there’s a unique magic in every story waiting to be discovered." I replied with a composed yet warm tone.

"Hmm, so I guess you’re politely telling me to be quiet," she teased, a shared chuckle breaking the momentary silence between us.

Suddenly, Eila’s tone turned urgent, a note of seriousness colouring her voice. "There’s something crucial you need to know," she said, her words now carrying a weight of importance.

I looked up, surprised by the seriousness in her tone.

"What’s going on, Eila? Why do you look so concerned?"

Eila took a deep breath before speaking, her voice carrying a blend of seriousness and reassurance. "Each year, there’s an initiation night held on the football field for the incoming freshmen. It may seem thrilling, but sometimes, there is a chance of some ragging taking place tonight. I want to ensure you are prepared and informed about your rights," she explained, her tone focused and supportive.

"Ragging is strictly prohibited in our college. You are not obliged to comply with anything that makes you uncomfortable, and you have the absolute right to refuse," she emphasized, continuing with unwavering conviction.

In the quaint town of Avalora, a peculiar tradition thrived within the walls of RSS. With the dawn of each new academic session, senior students engaged in what they termed the "initiation night." It entailed a series of challenges and ragging activities imposed on the freshmen, all orchestrated on the school's expansive field. This clandestine tradition had persisted for years, evading the vigilant gaze of the faculty, she explained. The seniors viewed initiation night as a rite of passage, a way to toughen up the newcomers and establish a sense of camaraderie. However, what started as harmless pranks soon escalated into humiliating and degrading activities, causing distress among the freshmen.

"When I was a freshman last year, I refused to do the 'pregnant lady' ramp walk. As a consequence, I spent my entire first night at RSS washing all the senior girls' dirty undergarments in the dorm," Eila recounted, her words causing my brows to furrow with concern. "Oh no, that sounds dreadful. What should I do?" I asked, feeling a sense of worry creeping in.

"What if I skip the initiation tonight and find somewhere safe, like the library?" I suggested, hoping for an alternative.

Eila's voice carried a hint of apprehension as she replied, "If I were you, I wouldn't risk making that choice."

"But why?" I pressed for an explanation.

Her reply was tinged with gravity, "You wouldn't want to face a boycott or endure the relentless torment of influential seniors for the next three years of their stay." Her words sliced through the air, sharp and merciless.

Fear gnawed at me as I contemplated what the night might hold in store.

3

An Enigma

BANG! BANG! The loud knocking reverberated through my room, jolting me awake from a deep slumber. Groggy and disoriented, I stumbled out of bed, trying to comprehend the urgency of the situation.

The moment I opened the door, Eila stood before me, her expression a mix of concern and urgency. "Why aren't you ready yet? The initiation's starting, and you cannot miss it!" Her words rushed out, impatience edging her voice.

Rubbing my eyes, I battled to shake off the remnants of sleep. Anxiety and uncertainty flooded over me. "I-I'm not sure if I can handle it," I confessed, my voice barely audible. The looming initiation night had cast a shadow of dread over my entire day. The idea of navigating a crowded event with my introverted tendencies felt daunting and terrifying.

Eila's nod was firm, her energy unwavering. "You can! We need to get to the field. Seniors and freshmen should be there by now. Latecomers face penalties. Trust me, you don't want that on your very first day."

Unenthusiastically and filled with fear, I quickly changed and reluctantly joined Eila as we headed out.

The setting sun casts long, dramatic shadows across the field, creating a captivating play of light and dark. The boundary lines, usually stark white, now appear as faint, ghostly outlines against the darkening grass, adding an aura of mystery to the scene. The goalposts stand tall and proud, their frames casting elongated shadows as the sun sinks lower in the sky. The nets, gently swaying in the evening breeze, seem to catch the fading light, creating a shimmering effect. Nestled between rolling hills and lush greenery, the RSS stood tall, not just as an educational institution, but as a beacon of football excellence. Over the years, it had proudly boasted the region's finest football team, some of whom had even secured spots in the national football team, earning a reputation that echoed far beyond the town's borders. Football at RSS was not merely a sport; it embodied a way of life. The school's passionate coaches, dedicated staff, and talented students came together to create a powerhouse of football prowess. The players were not just teammates; they were a family, bound by their love for the game and their shared goal of reaching new heights.

In the dim glow of the tranquil evening, I hesitated as I walked towards the football field. The rumours about these events had painted them as intimidating, and I was unsure if I dared to step on that very ground. Just as I was about to turn away, Eila, appeared at my side, her eyes sparkling with determination.

I could also see a group of apprehensive fellow mates making their way toward the bustling field. Nervous whispers floated through the air as they approached the gathering of seniors, their faces etched with a mix of excitement and uncertainty.

Under the vast expanse of the evening sky, a group of spirited seniors had gathered on the football field at RSS, their faces alight with mischievous excitement. They were eagerly awaiting the arrival of the new juniors, and their plans were far from ordinary. These seniors had a reputation for their playful nature and a knack for pranks.

As they huddled together, a twinkle in their eyes revealed their shared sense of adventure. With a commanding presence, Sara, a senior known for clever wit, stepped forward. Her voice carried across the field as she addressed the juniors, "Alright, everyone, let us give the juniors a warm, albeit unconventional, welcome to the RSS family. Gather in lines, girls on one side and boys on the other. We're going to introduce you properly to the RSS family."

The juniors, though a bit apprehensive, followed the instructions, forming neat lines divided by gender. The seniors, standing at the front, observed the organized formation with a nod of approval.

Zane, another senior, joined Sara. " Well, look who we have here, the fresh-faced juniors! I bet none of you have anything interesting to say, but let us waste a moment anyway. Now, we will go down the lines, and each of you will introduce yourselves briefly."

Their expressions contorted into malicious grins as they initiated a tirade of mockery and insults directed at us.

Senior 1: (Sarcastically) "Well, well, look at the newbies on the block. Fresh, clueless juniors who think that just getting admission at RSS means they belong here. Time to test if they do. Don't you think it is fair?"

Senior 2: (Laughing) "Absolutely. Let us see if they can handle a bit of our 'welcoming'. Hey, you in ugly glasses! Come here!" (pointing finger).

Junior: (Nervously approaching) "Uh, hi, I'm Samuel."

Senior 1: (Sneering) "Oh, Samuel, is it? Well, Samuel, why don't you tell us your deepest, darkest secrets. Tell us your embarrassing stories. And don't you dare hold back." (dragging Samuel towards him by his hand)

Junior: (Stammering uncomfortably) "I... I don't have any dark secrets to share...."

Senior 2: (Mocking) "Oh, afraid already, are we? What kind of junior cannot handle a bit of fun? Speak up or face the consequences."

(Trying to protest) "Leave him alone! We are here to study, not be your toys for mockery," I interjected, my voice surprisingly firm amid the chaos.

Everyone turned to look at me, taken aback by the sudden assertiveness.

"Well, well, look what we have here," dripping with sarcasm. "A fresh little fish in our big, bad pond. What is your name, newbie?"

As the scene unfolded, a voice boomed from beyond the crowd, projecting with conviction. I moved in the direction of the voice, and there he was. I recognized him; he was the ruthless basher I had seen outside the dormitory earlier in the morning.

An electric tingle surged down my spine, causing goosebumps to rise on my arms as if the air itself crackled with historic energy. It was an inexplicable sensation, a sign that I had stumbled upon something extraordinary—an enigmatic revelation that promised to alter the course of history.

Beneath the star-studded sky, he stood in an aura of confidence and charm. His athletic physique spoke volumes of unwavering dedication and countless hours devoted to the gym, hinting at both power and nimbleness. His posture exuded a natural elegance, a testament to years of vigorous physical pursuits.

His wavy hair, a shade of chestnut brown, was tousled in a way that made it look effortlessly stylish. It fell just above his eyebrows, adding to his rugged charm. His eyes, the colour of a deep hazel, were bright and expressive, reflecting his enthusiasm for life. They held a spark of determination, revealing a relentless drive for success.

His chiselled jawline highlighted his facial contours, complemented by a light stubble that added a hint of maturity to his appearance. His frequent smirk, an emblem of his reckless and somewhat arrogant demeanour, though irksome, held a strangely captivating and contagious allure. Clad in relaxed sports attire, he moved effortlessly, displaying a profound connection with his physique. Whether dashing across the field or strolling casually, his motions exuded a natural elegance, a testament to his athletic finesse.

Beyond his rebellious exterior lay an irresistible charm, an enigma that caused even the most rational hearts to quicken their beat. He epitomized both danger and desire, an enthralling puzzle that left a trail of fascination wherever he ventured.

Lost in the labyrinth of my thoughts, I failed to register the words as he spoke. My mind, entangled in its musings, had momentarily detached from the present. It was then that a stern voice pierced through my reverie, snapping me back to reality.

"Hey! Are you even listening?" the voice, tinged with irritation, reached my ears. I looked up to see his furrowed brows and the disappointment etched across his face.

My cheeks flushed with embarrassment.

All eyes landed on me as the ruthless basher vociferated pointing in my direction. I was so lost describing the irresistible devil that I lost track of what was being said.

I was in trouble.

"What on earth do you think you are?" His stern gaze bore into mine, demanding attention.

"Why don't you make an introduction?"

As I stood there, he advanced with a steady gaze, and a surge of inexplicable emotions swept through me. His annoyed tone sent shivers down my spine, evoking a mix of fear that left my soul simultaneously cold and yet ablaze. His presence was authoritative, his gaze penetrating and intense. The heat of the moment seemed to permeate my skin, bringing an unexpected warmth to my cheeks. The intensity of his scrutiny made my knees wobble as if the ground beneath me had momentarily turned unstable.

The closeness between us was charged with an electric intensity, the atmosphere crackling with an unseen force. My legs threatened to buckle under the weight of his presence as if his mere existence had the power to weaken my very core. A rush of heat surged through my veins, painting my cheeks with a rosy hue. It felt as though invisible flames danced beneath my skin, leaving me both invigorated and flustered.

His words lingered in the air, each passing moment amplifying the sound of my own heartbeats echoing loudly in my ears. There was an inexplicable yet palpable energy between us, a connection I struggled to comprehend fully. It felt as though his very presence had the ability to stir a swarm of butterflies in my stomach, heightening my awareness of his closeness and its impact on me.

Attempting to introduce myself felt like lifting a heavy burden, as if the weight of the past was tugging me backward, threatening to overshadow the present. The atmosphere grew stifling, and the burden of self-consciousness weighed heavily upon me.

"I... I... I'm... Saya... Sayami," I began, my voice catching, the familiar stutter resurfacing despite my efforts. Embarrassment flooded my cheeks, a blend of frustration and vulnerability overwhelming my senses. Throughout my childhood, I grappled with a stuttering issue, particularly when my emotions surged. Simple feelings of excitement, anger, or joy could trigger my speech impediment, causing me significant difficulty in expressing myself clearly. These overwhelming emotions tangled my words, leaving me feeling both frustrated and self-conscious. With time, I learned to navigate my stuttering through support, therapy, and patience.

"I see. Our queen newbie is a stutterer. And I don't understand your language. And I doubt any of us do," his eyes narrowed with disdain as my words stuttered, his tone laced with mockery. "Wow, can't even talk right, can you, Ms. Queen newbie? It's like listening to a broken record. Pathetic." His cruel remarks hung in the air, rendering me feeling small and exposed.

His humiliation was cutting, and the gazes around me felt like scrutinizing spotlights, heightening the pressure I already felt.

I stood on the verge of an emotional breakdown, uncertain whether this moment signalled the peak of adversity or merely the beginning of even more daunting challenges ahead.

4

Dance to the Dummy

Dark clouds loomed overhead, and a chilly wind rustled the leaves as the unsettling scene of mockery and humiliation unfolded. Standing in silence, I felt the heat of embarrassment radiating across my flushed cheeks.

A senior named Arin, notorious for his no-nonsense demeanour and sporadic rudeness, stepped forward, his stern and authoritative presence commanding attention. "Listen up, losers. We don't have time for your nonsense," he declared.

The junior students exchanged uneasy glances but remained attentive to his words. Arin pointed mockingly towards a chair, detailing their demands for an absurd dance routine. "The guys will dress as girls and perform a lap dance to the dummy seated there. But mind you, make it good or face the consequences."

"Ain't I right, Ayank?" he turned towards the ruthless basher, a devilish smirk playing across his lips. As they exchanged nods, their eyes gleaming mischievously, an unspoken understanding passed between them, sharing a conspiratorial moment that spoke volumes.

"And for the ladies, your task is to use the goalpost pole as a prop and perform a pole dance. Fail this, and there will be dire consequences. Your punishment? Cleaning this entire field until it shines brighter than your future," smirked Sia, adding a touch of disdain as she gestured toward the muddy ground.

Some of the junior students audibly gulped in response to her words.

Maya, notorious for her sharp tongue and quick temper, sneered, "I'd start brainstorming if I were you." A tense silence falls over the football field as Maya's harsh words hang in the air, leaving the juniors visibly shaken. Their eyes dart nervously between each other, uncertainty etched on their faces, silently vowing to avoid the dreaded penalty.

As I scanned the scene, the seniors exuded a mix of authority and curiosity, standing tall and forming an imposing barrier around the newcomers, evidently relishing the discomfort they were causing. However, amidst this disconcerting sight, my attention turned to Eila, standing behind her classmates. Her expression remained an impenetrable mask, void of any emotion, leaving me wondering whether she was complicit in the humiliation or if there was a reason preventing her from voicing opposition against it.

Amidst the uncertain whispers among the juniors, a voice cut through the hesitant murmurs, "What if some of us don't know how to dance?" However, within the sea of anxious faces, Maya noticed a larger boy who tentatively raised a question.

Maya's voice pierced through the assembly, carrying enough weight to capture everyone's attention. "Oh, look who's decided to voice their thoughts! Mr. 'Big Guy' here has something to say, huh? Hold on!"

She paused, her gaze fixed on the boy. "So, care to introduce yourself?"

Maya's firm tone lingered as she awaited a response. The boy, visibly anxious, managed to stutter out his name.

"I-I'm Thomas," he replied nervously. "Alright, Thomas. Since you're eager to contribute, let's see what you're made of. How about fifty laps around the football field? That might help you show some respect," she continued.

Reluctantly, Thomas commenced his laps around the football field as instructed. Sensing his unease, the other students exchanged concerned looks, yet the weight of Maya's demand lingered, compelling compliance.

Tension crackled in the air as the seniors persisted in their unkind behavior, casting discomfort among the students. Despite the fear gripping my heart, I couldn't remain a passive bystander to the seniors' victimization of my peers. Every fiber of my being revolted against the unfolding injustice. With quivering hands and a tremulous voice, I summoned the courage to speak out. "That's enough! This treatment is unacceptable. You can't continue to mistreat others like this. It's unjust and wrong," I asserted firmly.

A sudden hush descended upon the football field, the atmosphere heavy with tension. I could sense the weight of the stares, some filled with surprise, others with a glimmer of hope. The seniors, accustomed to unquestioned authority, appeared taken aback by my defiance.

"It involves all of us. We're a community, and our unity should uplift, not cause distress. I can't stand by and watch injustice," I continued, my voice growing firmer.

Startled by my sudden outburst, Ayank began striding toward me. Each step he took seemed purposeful, his gaze locking into mine with a blend of frustration, mischief, and authority. He approached with an air of command, his voice measured but forceful. "That's enough. Stop talking," he ordered.

His words sliced through the air, stifling the surrounding chatter into an uneasy silence. His expression shifted from surprise to resolute severity. His eyes bore into mine, his authority unquestionable as he remarked, "You seem to enjoy interrupting and questioning, don't you? Since you're the 'queen newbie,' you deserve a grand welcome."

"Why don't you go and teach him how to give a lap dance?" he sneered, pointing toward the pudgy boy who struggled to keep up, attempting to circle the football field.

Shocked by the devil's rude demand, I instinctively glanced at Eila. Her raised eyebrows hinted that I should comply, but despite the unspoken pressure, I held my ground. Taking a deep breath, I spoke firmly, "I believe in treating others with respect. If the boy wishes to learn to dance, I'd be more than willing to help him willingly and respectfully, not under duress."

A heavy silence hung in the air. My gaze swept across the faces before me. I could sense the struggle of Thomas, trudging around the vast field, showing signs of imminent exhaustion. But my attention reverted to the antagonist. He didn't seem pleased with my response.

"Don't you even think of defying us! This is your final opportunity to reconsider, or the next four years will become a living nightmare for you. You will be boycotted and nobody will dare challenge my authority. It's in your best interest not to go against us," the devil's advocate warned, his tone laced with a chilling edge.

Feeling the weight of his threat, I stood frozen for a moment, my mind racing with fear and uncertainty. The prospect of being boycotted, and ostracized from the community, loomed over me like a dark cloud. With a deep breath, I reluctantly nodded, my voice barely above a whisper as I agreed to comply.

As I moved towards the boy on the field, my steps felt heavy, burdened not just by the task at hand, but by the knowledge that I was succumbing to pressure and betraying my own beliefs. It was a painful decision, one made out of fear of the consequences that would follow if I refused to obey.

At that moment, I felt a mixture of anger, helplessness, and humiliation, but I also knew that survival sometimes meant making difficult choices. As I approached the struggling boy, my mind raced, hoping I could find a way to fulfil the task without demeaning him or compromising my values.

As I reluctantly began to instruct him, my words felt hollow and insincere. I couldn't shake the feeling of being reduced to a mere pawn, forced to act against my will. The weight of the situation pressed down on my shoulders, leaving me with a sense of powerlessness and a bitter taste of humiliation.

His tone dripped with rudeness as he barked out his command to Thomas. "Hey, you fatso! Remove the dummy and sit on the chair. Our Queen newbie will teach you how to give a lap dance," he ordered, his words laced with contempt.

Thomas, visibly flushed with embarrassment, hesitated before reluctantly obeying. As he shifted the dummy and sat down, I couldn't ignore the humiliation etched across his face. Witnessing his distress was agonizing, and a surge of sympathy coursed through me.

The ruthless basher redirected his attention towards me, his tone still harsh and condescending. "Now, you, teach him how to dance," he demanded.

Feeling overwhelmed, I slowly sank, resting on my knees. Tears welled up, blurring my vision. The weight of the humiliation was suffocating, weighing heavily on me, filling me with shame and despair.

"What's the holdup?" someone shouted from the onlookers.

The weight of the degrading situation pressed down on me, crushing my spirit. My heart raced, and a wave of dizziness washed over me. It felt as though the ground was slipping away beneath my feet. I clutched the chair's edge for support, fearing I might collapse under the intense pressure.

The rude demands, the condescending tone, and the humiliation of having to teach the fat boy how to dance in such a degrading manner became unbearable. Each word echoed in my ears like a relentless drumbeat, threatening to shatter my composure. The desire to escape, to run away from the piercing gazes and the harsh judgment, consumed me.

I closed my eyes, trying to steady my breathing, but the humiliation and frustration continued to well up inside me. It felt like a storm raging within, threatening to engulf me. At that moment, I wished for the strength to stand up, to defy the cruelty, but the fear of further humiliation held me captive, rendering me powerless and on the verge of collapse.

With a trembling grip, I clung to the backrest of the chair, my fingers white-knuckled with shame and frustration. The weight of humiliation bore down on my shoulders, threatening to crush me beneath its burden. Unable to bear the public degradation any longer, I began to sway my body, my movements unsteady and erratic, mirroring the turmoil within.

Each sway was a desperate attempt to cope, a silent plea for the ground to open and swallow me whole, to escape the harsh judgment and the condescending eyes that bore into my soul. My face flushed with embarrassment, tears stinging the corners of my eyes as I tried to maintain some semblance of composure.

A droplet landed on my neck, followed by another, until the sky burst open, unleashing a deluge that saturated the earth. I lay there, rain soaking through my clothes, mingling with my tears. It felt as though the heavens wept in solidarity with my humiliation, the rain escalating into a heavy downpour. The once-crowded field now stood deserted around me. Voices vanished, replaced by the rhythmic drumming of raindrops on the ground. Everyone scattered for shelter, leaving me alone amidst the torrential downpour.

In the deluge, an odd sense of relief washed over me. The rain blended with my tears, cleansing the residue of shame and frustration. Despite the abandonment, in that solitude, amid the pouring rain, I discovered an unexpected solace. It was a moment of exposed vulnerability, yet paradoxically, it evoked a quiet strength within me.

A firm grip seized my right arm, pulling me upright from the rain-soaked ground. Disoriented and drenched, I turned to see him—his face partially shielded by the hood of his jacket—the ruthless basher and devil's advocate who had orchestrated the humiliation.

"The show is over. You will fall ill." His voice, though commanding, held a note of concern.

Despite his firm grip, I forcefully pulled my arm from his hold, fury bubbling within me. I squared my shoulders, locking eyes with him, my defiance evident. "I will manage just fine," I shot back, my voice edged with defiance. "I don't need your concern."

His demeanour remained stoic, the pressure of his grip on my arm intensifying, sending a jolt of pain through me. I winced but refused to yield. "Let go! I won't endure this treatment," I protested, my words met with silence. He disregarded my objections, unmoved by my protests.

My frustration surged, and my words dripped with exasperation. "You're not in charge of me. Don't dare speak to me like that. And why the sudden concern? Weren't you satisfied with the humiliation you caused just ten minutes ago?" My voice quivered, a mix of anger and distress taking hold.

He edged closer, his breath grazing my skin, his intense gaze locking onto mine. With a final, authoritative tone, he commanded, "Return to your dorm." His words lingered in the air, underscoring his dominance, yet I stood my ground in defiance. Despite the distress welling inside me, I refused to bow to intimidation.

"I will go when I want to," I asserted, determination firm in my voice, despite the turmoil of fear and anger within me. I refused to let his cruelty obliterate me, clutching onto the remnants of my pride and self-respect.

His unyielding dominance and disregard for my emotions heightened my frustration to its limit. I sensed I was confronting an obsessive and unrelenting force, and my tolerance reached its breaking point. Summoning a surge of determination, I forcefully pulled my arm away from his grip, disregarding the lingering pain. Without looking back, I swiftly turned and sprinted, my legs carrying me as fast as they could over the rain-soaked ground. Fueled by a surge of anger, the terrain became a blur beneath my feet. I had reached my limit with his domineering attitude and indifference—I was adamant about not subjecting myself to it any further.

5

Quintessential Bad Boy

I was jolted awake by a loud bang on the door, the sound echoing through the room. Confusion washed over me as I glanced at the clock and realized it was already afternoon. The sunlight streamed in through the curtains, casting a warm glow over my surroundings.

"You've been in there all day. Are you okay?" Eila's voice came from the other side of the door, her tone a mix of concern and impatience.

I rubbed my eyes, trying to shake off the remnants of sleep. As I got up, the events of the past day flooded back into my mind, reminding me of my self-imposed seclusion. With a heavy sigh, I made my way to the door, preparing to face the world outside, uncertain of what awaited me beyond that familiar threshold.

"What do you want, Eila? I don't want to talk to anyone. Just go away," I said, trying to close the door. Eila stepped in, stopping me from shutting it entirely. "Just wait, please. Hear me out, will you?" Her touch was gentle as she held onto my hand.

Her brow furrowed slightly as she sensed something was wrong. Her fingers lightly brushed my forehead, and her eyes widened in alarm. "You're burning up. We need to go to the infirmary," she urged with concern.

"I don't want .to go anywhere with you," I retorted, feeling resentful.

"I understand you're upset with me for not defending you when Ayank humiliated you. Please, come with me, and I will explain everything. Just come with me," she pleaded earnestly.

Lacking the energy to resist further, I relented and agreed.

As we walked down the hallway, my steps were unsteady, and my body felt weighed down by the fever's relentless grip. Despite my anger, I was grateful for her presence, her support a reassuring anchor in my time of need. In the infirmary, the nurse's experienced hands took over, tending to me with care and professionalism.

At that moment, I realized the depth of her friendship and concern. She had noticed my distress, acted swiftly, and provided the comfort and care I desperately needed. It was a reminder that sometimes, in the face of adversity, it's the kindness and compassion of a friend that can make all the difference.

"How did you get a fever?" she asked, her brow furrowed in worry.

Struggling to muster a smile amid my discomfort, I responded with a hoarse voice, "I ended up drenched in the rain after last night's absurdity." The memory of the sudden downpour and the chaos of that moment felt surreal in hindsight.

Her concern deepened, and she shook her head, a mixture of exasperation and empathy colouring her expression. "You always find yourself in some kind of trouble, don't you?" she remarked, a faint smile breaking through her worry.

I nodded, appreciating her presence deeply. Even in the haze of my fever, her concern and the warmth of her smile provided a reassuring comfort. It was a reminder that despite my sometimes reckless actions, there would always be someone caring and worrying about my well-being.

Feeling weak and dizzy, I struggled to maintain my balance. My steps faltered, and I began to slump, drained by the fever. Without a word, she instinctively reached out, gently taking hold of my arm to support my weight as we made our way slowly to the infirmary.

As we made our way to the infirmary, her attention shifted to me, a note of concern coloring her voice. "You should steer clear of Ayank," she cautioned, her words carrying a warning edge. "He's widely known as the college's quintessential bad boy and a notorious womanizer."

Eila took my right hand firmly, her grip unwavering. "He lives by his own set of rules, takes what he wants, and revels in his playboy lifestyle. Women practically flock to him; he's been involved with a significant number of the women at RSS. No one dares to challenge him. He thrives on confrontation."

"Why doesn't anyone oppose him? He's a threat!" I exclaimed, my voice edged with defiance, my anger evident.

"The issue is that his grandfather holds a crucial position within the founding committee," she explained. "The committee plays a significant role in the college's financial support, funding scholarships, research initiatives, infrastructure development, and other vital projects. These contributions enhance the college's reputation, attract more students, and foster partnerships with businesses and organizations."

"Furthermore, RSS boasts the state's top football team, led by Ayank. He's an outstanding player, especially in football — perceptive, hardworking, meticulous, and relentless. Once he steps onto the field, he becomes an indomitable force, swiftly dominating his opponents. Ayank's proximity to the national football team selection has elevated his status within RSS, and his growing arrogance is palpable. While his talent on the field made him a star, it also seemed to inflate his ego, making him believe he was untouchable. Confronting him is akin to challenging a lion in its den—a risky endeavour with potentially dire consequences," she explained further.

"I'd advise you to keep your distance from him. Since your confrontation with him, he won't miss any chance to cause trouble for you," Eila added, casually shrugging.

Her words made me pause, and I couldn't ignore the weight of her words. I had witnessed Ayank's propensity for trouble on two separate occasions in a single day. His ties to a powerful figure within the college administration only complicated matters further. It was a stark reminder that sometimes, taking the path of least resistance was the safest choice, especially when dealing with individuals whose behaviour posed significant concerns.

As her words settled in, I felt a mixture of frustration and resignation. It was a bitter truth to swallow, but her caution was undeniable. At that moment, I made a silent vow to tread carefully, to navigate the complexities of college life with caution, and to choose my battles wisely, knowing that the consequences of defiance could be far-reaching.

"Let's shift gears here. There's plenty else going on at RSS to focus on. Speaking of which, at the end of this month, we seniors are organizing a '70s retro-themed Opening Gala for the freshmen at the convention center," she mentioned, attempting to redirect our conversation and uplift my mood.

The news didn't bring comfort. Following the humiliation from the previous night, social gatherings felt like a nightmare for someone like me—more introverted and less inclined to outgoing events.

"I won't be going," I responded promptly.

"Why not? It's a chance for freshmen and second-year students to mingle. It's an opportunity for making friends, dancing, having some drinks, and enjoying. It's one of the most anticipated nights at RSS. But to join, you will need a dance partner," she explained.

"Fine. I will skip it then," I replied, my voice holding a hint of relief, trying to find an excuse to opt-out.

Eila grinned, countering, "You know, it's mandatory for freshmen. Plus, everyone gets assigned a dance partner, including you."

A heavy sigh escaped me as I glanced helplessly out the window. The sun dipped low, painting the sky in fiery reds, evoking an eerie sense of foreboding. The crimson hues seemed to foretell an inevitable clash. "Facing Ayank again... I dread it," I murmured to myself, a cloud of apprehension enveloping my thoughts. I had arrived at RSS with aspirations of success, but now, I doubted whether Ayank would permit it. Uncertainty lingered, casting a shadow of worry over my ambitions.

6

Spirit of the 70s

Leaving my dorm, I could hear the distant echoes of booming music growing louder and clearer with each step I took toward the party venue. The infectious beats of "Something" by The Beatles filled the air, setting the tone for the night's festivities.

Before me stood the colossal, pristine edifice, its sheer size and grandeur commanding attention. Towering banners, adorned with the emblem of RSS, gracefully swayed between the stately pillars that framed the entrance. The vibrant crowd, buzzing with chatter and excitement, flowed towards the building. Joy and anticipation radiated from every attendee, setting the tone for an exhilarating night ahead. It was unmistakably the convention centre, the epicentre of the evening's festivities.

Under the twilight sky of the college campus, vibrant lights flickered, casting a warm, nostalgic glow across the venue. A sense of anticipation filled the air as the meticulously arranged decorations transformed the ordinary space into a vibrant tableau from the past. Strings of multicoloured fairy lights hung overhead, reflecting in the eyes of the excited freshmen.

Contemplating the attendance of my classmates, I wondered if they had overcome the lingering apprehension from the initiation night or if their presence here was obligatory. Perhaps the tension between juniors and seniors had eased after the initiation event.

Despite my uncertainties, the atmosphere was adorned with radiant and cheerful expressions.

The music of the '70s filled the atmosphere, pulling everyone into an era of disco beats and rock anthems. Seniors, dressed in bell-bottoms, neon hues, and retro chic, welcomed the freshmen with infectious smiles, setting the tone for the night.

A checkerboard dance floor became the centre of attention, beckoning newcomers to showcase their moves. The walls were adorned with vintage movie posters and vinyl records, each telling a story from an era long past. Tables were laden with classic snacks and drinks, offering a taste of the past, while old arcade games in one corner brought out the competitive spirit among the attendees.

Laughter and excitement mingled with the timeless tunes, creating an atmosphere where generations seemed to blend seamlessly. Seniors guided the freshmen, sharing anecdotes from the past and making them feel like part of an extended family.

In the vibrant ambience of the 70s-themed party, I stepped into the spotlight wearing a dress borrowed from Eila herself, and I felt utterly transformed. The classic A-line silhouette gracefully embraced my curves, giving me a touch of vintage glamour from the bygone era. Crafted from a luxurious fabric with a subtle sheen, the dress boasted a rich midnight blue hue, reminiscent of the velvety night sky. Yet, it wasn't just a simple monochrome piece.

Intricate floral patterns in hues of gold, crimson, and emerald green adorned the dress, adding opulence and depth to the ensemble. The bodice featured a sweetheart neckline, delicately adorned with lace and sequin embellishments that glimmered under the soft disco lights, casting a subtle sparkle around me.

As I twirled, the layers of chiffon skirt gracefully flowed, each tier trimmed with delicate lace, infusing a vintage charm into every movement.

Completing the ensemble, I wore matching accessories that accentuated the retro vibe. Dainty white gloves, reaching just above my wrist, added a touch of sophistication to my look. My hair was elegantly styled into victory rolls, a classic nod to the era, and a vibrant red flower tucked behind one ear added a pop of colour. On my feet, I donned peep-toe heels in the same midnight blue shade, embellished with a small bow at the front, completing the ensemble with a perfect blend of vintage allure and contemporary style.

In this outfit, I felt like I had stepped out of a time machine, embracing the spirit of the 70s in every seam while adding my modern flair to the mix. In Eila's borrowed creation, I felt not just adorned, but transformed, embodying the free-spirited essence of the era and becoming a living testament to its timeless allure.

Despite having a plethora of excuses, she remained resolute in her insistence that I attend. She firmly believed that not attending would only lead to more trouble for me. I couldn't help but feel like a stranger in my skin. Confidence eluded me, and I harboured a sense of foreboding about the party. The memory of the last interaction event still haunted me, a vivid reminder of my previous humiliation.

As I contemplated the evening ahead, I couldn't help but silently plead for divine intervention, hoping that this time would be different.

I hadn't crossed paths with Ayank for the past one month. However, glimpses of him in random college spots like the cafeteria or school hallways sent me scurrying away, desperate to avoid any confrontation. Since our last encounter in the field, he had become a persistent presence in my thoughts.

My emotions towards him were a tumultuous blend of fury and irritation. He exuded arrogance, presumption, and a domineering attitude. His lack of respect for any human being was appalling, painting him as a mannerless and disgraceful individual. And yet, there was an undeniable allure about him, a dangerous magnetism that defied reason.

His handsome features, those broad shoulders, the infuriating smirk, mischievous deep hazel eyes, and that seductive voice all combined to create a devilish charm. It was infuriating how someone so infuriating could be so undeniably attractive.

Every night as I attempt to sleep, thoughts of him invade my mind, refusing to let go. His presence lingers an inescapable spell that wraps around my thoughts. Despite the embarrassment he caused me, I can't deny the strange energy, an inexplicable pull he exerts on me. The day I saw him on those grounds, he left something behind in me.

When everyone else had departed, I found myself drenched in the rain, utterly alone. Yet, he returned, or perhaps he had never left at all. His sudden reappearance, urging me to seek shelter, came after causing the most intense humiliation I had experienced. His actions, following such embarrassment, presented a baffling mystery that I couldn't begin to unravel. Yet, amidst it all, I find myself grappling with moral dilemmas, questioning how I could feel drawn to someone with such a questionable character.

My thoughts were abruptly interrupted by the ringing of my phone, causing me to startle.

"Did you return to the dorm?" Eila's voice came through the phone, loud and urgent, even before I could greet her with a hello.

"I just stepped out for some fresh air," I responded, trying to sound casual, my voice competing with the thumping music playing in the background.

"Come quickly; it's about to begin," she urged before abruptly ending the call.

I tried to calm the whirlwind of thoughts in my mind. After all, he was Ayank, the irresistible enigmatic bad boy of RSS.

ᑭᑭᑭ

7

Opening Gala

As the night progressed, the dance floor came alive with colourful outfits, swaying bodies, and infectious energy. The spirit of camaraderie and shared nostalgia permeated the air, making the retro-themed opening gala a night to remember, a bridge between the past and the promising future of the freshmen in the vibrant tapestry of college life.

In the dimly lit room, a sense of unease settled as I found myself alone, contemplating my thoughts. It was a place of solitude, a sanctuary for my introspection, or so I thought.

"Would you mind dancing?" A feeble voice amidst loud music came from behind. I was unsure if what I heard was right and if someone was offering me a dance, so I turned around.

The dimmed lights in the room cast a soft glow, and the golden flecks floating around from the disco ball painted tiny stars on the walls. The pulsating beats of the music filled the room, and most were lost in their rhythm, swaying and dancing to their heart's content.

As I mulled over my inner demons, a sudden, chilling presence made my skin prickle, and a shiver ran down my spine.

And there he stood, shrouded in darkness, his eyes gleaming with an otherworldly intensity. It was Ayank, a name that had haunted my nightmares and stirred my deepest fears. He was the embodiment of all that was sinister and malevolent, a figure I had hoped never to encounter.

My voice quivered as I uttered his name in disbelief, "Ayank." His sinister smile widened, revealing a row of sharp, glistening teeth. He took a slow, deliberate step toward me, his presence exuding a palpable malevolence that seemed to seep into every corner of the room.

At that moment, I realized that my thoughts had summoned this unholy presence, and there was no escaping the dark consequences of my contemplations. The room felt like a prison, and Ayank, the warden of my own personal hell.

Amidst the vibrant colours and boisterous laughter filling the room, it seemed that he walked straight out of a 70s movie scene, embodying the spirit and vivacity of the era. With wavy chestnut hair reaching just past his ears, he exuded a natural charisma that made heads turn.

He wore a crisp white shirt with exaggerated pointed collars peeking out beneath a velvet blazer in deep maroon. The jacket was adorned with vintage gold buttons that gleamed every time they caught the light. Tucked into a pair of high-waisted bell-bottom trousers in a rich shade of brown, his ensemble perfectly captured the essence of the era.

Around his neck, a bold pendant hung on a gold chain, resting against his chest, a nod to the bold accessories that were a staple of the time. His feet were encased in polished platform shoes, elevating his height and adding to the overall flamboyance of his look.

His eyes, outlined subtly with kohl, gleamed with excitement and anticipation for the night ahead. As he moved with confidence, the musky scent of his cologne left a lingering trail, reminiscent of the nostalgic fragrances of the 70s. Every gesture and every step he took was filled with an authentically retro flair.

His voice, eerily calm and familiar, reverberated in the air, sending shivers down my spine. The casual tone of his words contrasted sharply with the weight they carried. I blinked, attempting to compose myself despite the deep sense of unease that accompanied his presence.

Memories began to flicker, shadows of past events dancing at the periphery of my mind. The dim lighting didn't help as I squinted, trying to discern his features more clearly. Those deep-set eyes, the way he tilted his head slightly — it was all too hauntingly familiar.

A cold bead of sweat trickled down my temple. The ambience of the room, which moments ago felt lively and electrifying, now felt stifling. The background music seemed distant, conversations around me blurred into incomprehensible murmurs, and time felt suspended.

"What do you want?" I managed to choke out, my voice barely a whisper.

He leaned in closer, his eyes locked onto mine, searching, probing. "I'd like to dance with you," he stated.

The weight of our shared history, the unsaid words, and unresolved tensions hung heavy between us. The past had a way of catching up, and it seemed, today, it had caught up with me.

His presence never failed to rattle me. Gathering my wits, I fought back the frenzy of emotions. This time, I vowed not to yield (although, perhaps I might). Attempting to sound indignant, I retorted, "And what on earth makes you think I would dance with you?"

"Because I am your designated dance partner," he replied confidently.

At the party, juniors were paired with senior dance partners, a fact I had forgotten to confirm beforehand. The realization hit me, making me feel utterly foolish.

"What if I don't want to dance with you?" I replied, my tone laced with anger. I was still nursing the wounds of humiliation from the very first day, feeling dejected and infuriated by his actions.

The ambience was wrapped in a soft, dim glow, matching the slow tempo of the music that filled the air. There I stood, barely an inch away from my adversary, the devil basher who both terrified and intrigued me. His intentions were clear, conveyed through his confident gestures and movements.

As usual, he disregarded my protests and objections. Before I could utter another word, his left hand found its place on my waist, pulling me closer, while his right hand delicately cradled my left, resting it upon his shoulder. I dared not meet his gaze, avoiding those deep hazel eyes that concealed countless secrets. The thought of locking eyes with him felt akin to plunging into a bed of fragrant roses intertwined with thorns—a temptation too risky to entertain. His touch ignited a rush of emotions, setting my heart into a frenzied rhythm. Drawing me nearer, we moved in sync to the melody of "Close to You" by The Carpenters.

In profound silence, his grip strong and assured, I could sense the power and gentleness in his touch. I felt the warmth and tenderness of his body as he held me close. His breaths were deep and heavy, matching the rhythm of our unspoken connection.

His hands, resting on my back, began to draw me nearer, and my hand, previously on his shoulder, gradually made its way to his chest. In that suspended moment, time seemed to stand still, and I could feel the rhythm of his heart pulsating within his masculine chest. Overwhelmed, I closed my eyes, succumbing to the intoxicating sensation. It was an emotion unlike any I had ever experienced before.

He gently cradled my chin, a silent request for me to meet his gaze as I had been avoiding direct eye contact. His touch held my face, and I yielded, opening my eyes, and found myself lost in his intense gaze, a place where words ceased and emotions spoke volumes.

"Come with me," he whispered softly into my ear, a request laden with mystery. I didn't know where we were headed, but my consent was evident in my eyes as he still held my hand.

He gently steered us away from the lively atmosphere of the convention centre, leading the way toward the shadowy embrace of the woods. The school, perched on vast grounds, was a solitary structure encircled by an expanse of dense forests and woods stretching to the outskirts. Beyond the trees lay a quiet world, with residential areas distant, at least 50 miles away.

"Where are we going?" I inquired, curiosity getting the better of me.

"Come with me," he whispered into my ears.

"No! I am not going anywhere with you, Ayank," I declared firmly, trying to pull my hand away from his grasp.

He implored, "Trust me and come with me," his words laden with sincerity, urging me to put my faith in him.

Uncertain of our destination, I yielded to temptation. His grip on my hand remained firm as he led me out of the bustling crowd.

The atmosphere was shrouded in an aura of mystique as we ventured deeper into the darkness of the woods. Throughout our silent journey, I couldn't help but wonder about the destination he had in mind, a mystery that hung in the air like an unanswered question. In that moment, I found myself entrusting Ayank, my hand firmly clasped in his, as we ventured deeper into the wilderness, the unknown path before us sparking a mix of excitement and trepidation. As I walked away from the convention centre, a chilling breeze swept through the air, causing me to shiver in the dress I was wearing - a crisp embrace that whispered of the coming winter.

After a fifteen-minute uphill trek through the dense woods, we finally reached the peak where the heavens seemed to embrace the river below. The sight that greeted us was nothing short of picturesque, a scene so breathtakingly beautiful that I felt as if I had stepped into a different world.

Above us, the night sky was adorned with countless stars, illuminated by the soft glow of the full moon. Their shimmering light cascaded down, delicately touching the surface of the crystal-clear river that lay before us. The river, though turbulent, mirrored the celestial display above, its rippling waters creating a mesmerizing reflection of the starlit sky.

At that moment, a profound sense of tranquillity washed over me, leaving me awestruck and utterly speechless. The sheer magnificence of the scene stole my words, and for the first time, I felt an overwhelming sense of peace and self-reflection.

"Sayami," Ayank's voice broke the silence, a gentle revelation piercing the stillness of the night, "this place is my hidden sanctuary. I come here when I'm weighed down by sorrow or disappointment. What you're witnessing tonight is a rare sight, and you're lucky to experience it."

My gaze involuntarily shifted towards this man who appeared both enigmatic and strangely familiar, a puzzle I couldn't decipher. In that fleeting moment, a serene expression graced his face, a departure from the devilish image I had painted of him. An unexpected gentleness replaced the imagined ferocity in his eyes. For the first time, I sensed an unfamiliar warmth and a comforting embrace of security. The night, once daunting, now possessed a different allure.

In the stillness of that moment, the world around us faded into insignificance. The rustling leaves and the distant sounds of the night seemed muted, leaving only Ayank and me under the enchanting canvas of stars. His revelation about this secret sanctuary had softened the edges of my perception of him, unveiling a vulnerability I hadn't seen before. Despite my initial reluctance, a strange sense of trust began to weave its way into my thoughts, entwined with the beauty of the secluded spot and the unexpected tranquillity that had settled over me.

"Why did you bring me here? Secret places are meant to be kept secret," I blurted out, my impatience getting the better of me. I couldn't fathom why the same man who seemed to derive pleasure from bullying me had chosen to reveal his most intimate sanctuary.

He released a long, weary sigh, his eyes distant as if lost in the depths of memory, "This is where my mom used to bring me, a haven from the abuse and bullying my dad subjected us to when he came home drunk. She was a strong woman, always fighting for us."

I stood in astonishment, both at his revelation and the unexpected trust he was extending to me. Why was he sharing such a deeply personal part of his life? What was it about me that made him open up in this way? A whirlwind of questions churned in my mind, and I found myself tightening my grip on his hand, a silent reassurance that I was there, listening, willing to understand the complexities of his past.

In that moment, I instinctively tightened my grip on his hand, the same hand he hadn't let go of since we left the dance floor. The gesture was my silent attempt to offer comfort and understanding.

"She was?" I inched a few steps closer to him, my curiosity piqued. Attempting to establish eye contact, I searched for his gaze, but he continued to gaze skyward as if lost in the tapestry of stars above.

"One day I woke up, and she was gone," he said softly, his voice laced with pain. "She left a letter, explaining that she couldn't endure the abuse and violence inflicted by my dad any longer. In her escape, she left me behind too," his words hung heavy in the air, echoing the ache of abandonment.

"Every day, she fought for us," he continued, his voice now carrying both sorrow and the weight of a heart-wrenching past. "But one day, she lost. I was just twelve when she fled during one of their relentless fights. I watched her walk away from my bedroom window, assuming she was out for a walk and would return. But she didn't. I didn't realize she was gone forever until the next day when I overheard my dad talking to my grandpa. I believed she loved me. If she did, how could she not think about me? How could she leave me too?" he confessed, the burden of that traumatic memory hanging heavily between us.

A sudden pang of empathy pierced my heart, and I could feel the weight of his pain. "I'm really sorry, Ayank. I shouldn't have asked you about this. I've invaded your personal pain, and for that, I am deeply regretful," I said, my voice heavy with remorse for my thoughtless curiosity. The weight of my words hung in the air, and I felt an overwhelming sense of guilt. "I should leave now," I added, feeling like an intruder in his private world. The remorse in my heart was deep, and I couldn't help but wish I could undo the pain my questions had inadvertently caused.

I gently withdrew my hands from his, intending to step back, but before I could move, his voice, unusually soft, called out, "Please stay, Sayami. Don't go."

The sheer request from Ayank, the boy I had deemed a devil, left me utterly amazed. I hesitated, my movements frozen in response to his unexpected plea. His cold hands found their way back into mine, and oddly, my heart didn't race; instead, it seemed to settle, as if finding solace in his touch.

Slowly, I turned around, my eyes meeting his. In those hazel depths, I felt myself getting lost, drawn into a spell that seemed to wrap around me, pulling me into a realm of enchantment and desire. His eyes held a power, an allure that bewitched me every time I gazed into them, carrying me away into a land of blissful ecstasy.

He inched closer, his intentions unmistakable, his eyes brimming with desire. His hand found its place on my waist, firm yet gentle, pulling me closer to him. The air between us crackled with an electrifying tension as if the universe itself was holding its breath in anticipation. His eyes, intense and tender, bore into mine, and I could feel the warmth of his breath, soft and tantalizing, against my lips. Time seemed to stand still, the world around us fading into insignificance. We were suspended at that moment, on the verge of a kiss that promised to be more than just a meeting of lips; it was a convergence of souls, a silent confession of emotions that words could never capture. Just as our lips were about to meet, a flash of Eila's warning raced through my mind, jolting me into caution. I moved back suddenly, breaking the intimate moment, my heart pounding with a mixture of desire and apprehension, my instinct urging me to tread carefully.

I abruptly pulled away from his proximity, my heart hammering in a chaotic mix of attraction and caution. Without looking back, I turned and sprinted back toward the convention centre. Confusion gripped me, urging me to escape the tumultuous emotions.

The dance party was in full swing as I rejoined, desperately seeking refuge in the crowd. I grabbed a drink and downed it, the liquid burning my throat as I attempted to drown my inner turmoil. With every sip, the world around me blurred, and soon, I felt as if I might lose consciousness.

My attempts to call Eila only heightened my panic when I realized my phone had been lost in the woods. Determined to leave, I stumbled my way towards the exit. Suddenly, everything went black as I stepped out of the convention centre, succumbing to the overwhelming rush of emotions and alcohol.

♡♡♡

8
Ayank's POV

Ayank's POV:

In the dim moonlight, I watched as Sayami hurried away from me, disappearing into the depths of the night. As she vanished into the distance, I felt a pang of longing I couldn't quite place. Confusion wrestled with desire inside me, leaving me unsettled. A part of me wanted to follow, to understand what had transpired between us, but another part, the more rational one, held me back.

For a moment, I stood there, torn between chasing after her and letting her go. I clenched my fists, trying to comprehend the whirlwind of emotions she had stirred within me. The intensity of her gaze and the warmth of her touch all lingered in my mind, clouding my thoughts.

There was an inexplicable draw in her defiance, in the unwavering determination that fueled her stand for what was right. Her vocal stance against injustice held a magnetic power, one that I found irresistibly alluring. Despite my usual detached demeanour, there was something about her, something deep and compelling, that made me want to understand her more, to unravel the layers beneath her strong facade. It was a curiosity I couldn't ignore, a pull that seemed to defy all logic.

The rush of intense emotions overwhelmed me, drowning rationality in a sea of compelling impulses. I found myself unable to resist the urge, an unexplainable force pushing me to go after her. It was as if an invisible thread connected us, tugging at my very core, urging me to bridge the distance between us and delve deeper into the enigma that was Sayami.

I hurriedly followed her, my steps echoing in the night as I ventured into the darkness before reaching the convention centre. I observed her weakening, her steps faltering as she left the party, likely headed towards her dorm room. As I turned a corner, I saw her, just a few meters away, collapsing to the ground. Panic gripped me, and I rushed to her side, concern etched deep into my features. The pounding of my heart was a cacophony in my ears, matching the urgency of my movements. My concern overpowered any logical reasoning, and I couldn't leave her in that vulnerable state.

With utmost care, I scooped her up, her slender form feeling fragile yet oddly resilient in my arms. Without a second thought, I carried her towards my grandfather's private residence, a secluded haven nestled within the heart of the campus. The residence, a sanctuary rarely occupied, stood as a silent witness to the passing days of the college year. As I entered the elegantly adorned living room, I gently laid her down on a plush couch, her pale face highlighted by the dim glow of the room's ambient light. For a moment, I studied her, captivated by the delicate vulnerability she exuded. Her unconscious form seemed fragile yet resilient, and a strange sense of protectiveness washed over me.

I covered her with a soft blanket, the worry etched on my face softening into a subtle, unseen expression of care. The night was quiet around us, the silence broken only by the faint sounds of nature outside the window. As I kept a watchful eye on her, myriad emotions swirled within me, leaving me both bewildered and strangely enchanted by the enigmatic girl lying before me.

I couldn't help but watch her sleep peacefully on the couch. In the soft glow of the room's dim light, her features were delicately highlighted, casting a gentle radiance on her slumbering form. Her hair, a cascade of midnight black, spilt over the pillow, framing her delicate face like a silken veil. Each strand seemed to have a mind of its own, dancing with the softest breeze, as if echoing the untamed spirit that dwelled within her. As she slept, her breathing was serene, her lashes casting delicate shadows on her cheeks, adding to her enchanting aura. I remember the initiation night vividly, the first time I gazed into her captivating, big eyes. They were a profound shade of mysterious brown, resembling pools of unwavering determination.

Her lips curved ever so slightly, held a tranquil smile as if she were in the midst of a pleasant reverie. Her presence exuded a quiet strength, a sense of resilience that drew me in. There was an undeniable beauty in her vulnerability, a beauty that transcended the physical, seeping into the very core of her being. Every inch of her skin seemed like a canvas, an ethereal blend of silk and moonlight, enchanting to the touch.

Yet, it was not just her physical attributes that drew my attention. Her features, though delicate, held a certain strength, a reflection of the stubborn spirit that resided within her. It was the way she held herself, even in sleep – a subtle defiance etched into her every feature. Despite her stubbornness, there was a vulnerability about her, a fragility that made her all the more enchanting.

My internal turmoil only deepened as I grappled with my unexpected feelings for her. Why was I so drawn to her, captivated by both her stunning beauty and her unwavering commitment to what was right? I had always prided myself on being emotionally detached, on not forming attachments after the devastating loss of my family. Vulnerability and emotions were things that infuriated me; they were weaknesses I had learned to shut off.

But this girl was different. There was something about her presence, her aura, that stirred the dormant emotions within me. From the very instant I laid eyes on her on that field, it felt as though she held the power to awaken emotions I believed were long buried within me. This realization only fueled my frustration. I resented the way she made me feel, how she cracked the armour I had so carefully constructed around my heart.

To regain control, to assert my dominance over my own emotions, I lashed out at her the initiation night on the field. I sought to humiliate her, thinking it might grant me some semblance of satisfaction, a twisted way to reclaim the power I felt slipping away. But instead of satisfaction, I was met with an overwhelming wave of guilt and shame. I was appalled by my actions, regretting the way I had treated her.

Yet, despite my attempts to push her away, my feelings for her persisted, refusing to be ignored. I was left grappling with the chaos of emotions she had ignited within me, questioning everything I thought I knew about myself. The invisible walls I had built around myself seemed fragile in the face of her stubborn determination and unwavering spirit.

A mix of emotions stirred within me, each one vying for dominance, something unspoken and vulnerable, an emotion I was unaccustomed to. I felt a strange protectiveness wash over me, an urge to shield her from the world's cruelties. Simultaneously, there was a pang of guilt, a recognition of the turmoil I inadvertently brought into her life. Yet, amidst it all, there was an undeniable attraction, a pull that defied logic.

The internal battle waged fiercely within me. As much as I longed to let her in, to share the depth of my emotions, I knew the perilous path such closeness could lead us down. Allowing her to get closer meant exposing her to the chaos of my world, a world I believed would only hurt her. I couldn't deny the inexplicable connection I felt towards Sayami, yet I couldn't let her get too close. I feared that the scars and darkness that clung to me would only end up hurting her in the end.

♡♡♡

9

Grandpa's Residence

With heavy eyes and a throbbing head, I stirred awake to a ray of unwelcome sunshine that fell across my face. The brightness was jarring, intensifying the pounding ache in my head. As I attempted to gather my thoughts, I slowly became aware that something was amiss. This wasn't my bed, and the surroundings were unfamiliar.

Panic gripped me like icy fingers around my heart. I strained my memory, attempting to piece together the fragments of the previous night. Flashes of a dance party, Ayank's enigmatic eyes, and a sense of disorientation washed over me. It was a struggle, akin to assembling a puzzle with missing pieces.

The pieces of the puzzle slowly started to fit together in my mind as I recalled the hazy fragments of the previous night. I vaguely remembered Ayank's strong arms enveloping me, lifting me off my feet as the world around me blurred into darkness.

This realization hit me like a freight train, jolting me awake from the remnants of sleep. The room, bathed in the soft morning light, felt alien and yet oddly familiar. My heart pounded in my chest like a frantic caged bird, its wings beating against the bars of my ribcage.

"No," I whispered to myself, hoping against hope that this was all a nightmare, a figment of my exhausted imagination. But the reality of Ayank's place, the subtle scent of his cologne that lingered in the air, told a different story. Panic clawed at my throat, threatening to suffocate me.

Unable to contain the surge of fear, I let out a piercing scream, the sound reverberating through the room. It was a desperate cry, a plea for escape from a situation that seemed to spiral out of my control.

I saw Ayank rush into the room, his expression a mix of concern and unease.

"Good morning, you're up! I made some breakfast for you," he greeted, holding a tray, his attempt to ease the tension, though it only seemed to exacerbate my distress.

"No, I don't want your breakfast. I want to leave," I protested, my voice trembling yet resolute. Pushing the tray away, I resisted every gesture.

Amid the overwhelming emotions and my attempt to walk toward the exit, striving to put more distance between Ayank and me, I hurried with haste. However, in my rush, I lost my balance and tumbled off the edge, landing on the floor with a heavy thud. Pain surged through me, but I gritted my teeth, determined not to show any vulnerability.

Ayank's frustration ignited, his patience wearing thin. "Why are you being so difficult? Can't you just accept my help?" he snapped, his tone laced with exasperation.

"What does it matter to you?" I retorted, my anger mingled with bewilderment. "Why did you bring me here? Why am I in your bed?" My voice escalated, reflecting the turmoil in my thoughts. "And you're not exactly the type to lend a hand, especially after all the embarrassment you caused me—and relished," I added with bitter indignation.

Ayank stood at the doorway, releasing a deep sigh, an attempt to diffuse the tension in the room. His voice, a soothing contrast to the whirlwind of thoughts in my head, carried a gentle tone as he began to speak. "Sayami, I need you to listen carefully," he said, his eyes reflecting both concern and understanding. "Last night, I found your phone that you dropped, so I came to return it. As I was heading towards your dorm, I stumbled upon you staggering from the party, clearly intoxicated and in no condition to reach your dorm safely. You collapsed, and I couldn't just leave you alone, especially in that state."

"Why should I listen to you?" my frustration bubbled over, my eyes flashing with indignation. My head was spinning, not just from the remnants of the alcohol but from the weight of Ayank's words. "Why... Why did you help me?" I managed to stammer, my voice laced with confusion.

Ayank sighed, his gaze softening. "I'm aware that my behaviour towards you hasn't been ideal, but regardless of our differences, nobody deserves to be left alone in such a vulnerable state. It doesn't matter how much we clash, I couldn't just ignore your safety. So, I brought you here, to my grandpa's residence on campus. It's secluded, secure, and you could rest without any disturbances."

"But... why?" my voice cracked, emotions getting the better of me. "Why would you do that for me, especially after all the humiliation you caused?"

Ayank hesitated, his expression vulnerable momentarily before looking away as if searching for the right words. "I might not like you, Sayami, but I don't want any harm to come your way. We might have our differences, but your safety matters, even to someone like me."

"And I noticed you were restless on the couch, and I was worried you might fall, so I moved you to my bed for your safety," he explained, a hint of a smirk playing on his lips.

In that fleeting moment, a blend of emotions engulfed me – gratitude, confusion, and a flicker of comprehension. Ayank, the enigmatic and often intimidating presence, had unveiled an unexpected side. Gazing into his eyes, I glimpsed a trace of sincerity, a glimmer of humanity that contradicted our tumultuous history.

"Thank you, I suppose," I murmured with a hint of disbelief, my tone tinged with conflicting emotions. "Your concern means something, Ayank, even if I'm not entirely sure what to make of it."

Ayank nodded, a silent acknowledgement passing between them. It seemed in that moment, amidst the uncertainty, a fragile bridge had been built.

"But you must promise not to disclose anything about this," his soft tone shifted into one of seriousness.

I stood there, momentarily dazed, trying to comprehend Ayank's request. A puzzled silence lingered before I finally voiced, "I'm not exactly keen on sharing details about last night," my tone was a mix of puzzlement and apprehension. "But what's the reason for keeping it all under wraps?"

He continued, "My reputation here is delicate, and having a girl in my grandpa's residence would tarnish it, for both me and my grandfather."

His words were like a sharp blade, piercing through my emotions and leaving me deeply wounded and offended. "If your reputation meant that much to you, you shouldn't have bothered to help," I shot back, my anger adding intensity to my retort.

I couldn't stand being near him another moment, the jumble of frustration, fury, and hurt pushing me toward the door. Tears blurred my vision as I stormed out, feeling a potent mix of regret, anger, and disillusionment. I berated myself for ever entertaining the notion that Ayank could be anything other than what he had shown himself to be.

10

A Collison of Desire

As the year-end exams loomed closer, I found solace amidst the library's hushed ambience. Surrounded by the scent of old books and the soft shuffle of pages, I buried myself in my studies, trying to drown out the ambient noise of rustling pages and hushed whispers around me. My phone buzzed, startling me out of my concentration. Glancing at the screen, I saw an unknown number. The message simply read, "Meet me in the old changing room behind the football field after classes. - Ayank."

How on earth did he get my number? I hadn't given it to him, and the unexpected intrusion left me both irritated and intrigued.

Finishing my studying, I couldn't shake off the nagging curiosity. Why did Ayank want to meet me? What could he possibly have to say that he couldn't discuss in public? The choice of location clearly suggests his concern about safeguarding his reputation. The very thought of it stoked the flames of my anger.

Months had passed without a single word exchanged between us, not since the morning after the opening gala. I had made a conscious effort to steer clear of him, avoiding any encounter at all costs.

Strangely, he hadn't attempted to reach out either, leaving a silence between us that seemed to echo the unspoken words and unresolved emotions that lingered in the air. Despite my annoyance, I found myself agreeing to meet him after the classes.

After the final bell rang, I made my way to the football field, my steps fueled by a mix of anger and curiosity, the chilly wind cutting through my coat. The old changing room stood there, once vibrant with the energy of athletes, now stood silent and abandoned. I pushed open the creaky door, finding Ayank standing in the dim light, looking both hesitant and remorseful.

"What do you want, Ayank?" I demanded, my voice sharper than I intended.

In the dim light of the old changing room, Ayank's eyes searched mine, "Sayami," he began, his tone hesitant, "I need you to understand what happened that night, the night I lashed out at you."

I watched him, my anger still simmering beneath the surface, but curiosity and concern tugging at my heartstrings. "What do you mean?" I asked, my voice softening despite my resolve to remain distant.

"The night I told you about my mom's departure... there is more to it." Ayank's voice was low, filled with a mixture of sorrow and determination.

"As I grew up, my parents' relationship was a tempest, fueled by my father's violent outbursts. As you know, when I was just a kid, my mother made the heart-wrenching choice to leave, abandoning both my father and me to a home filled with turmoil.

Growing up without a mother's care and under the shadow of my abusive father, I eventually fell victim to his violence. Three years after my mother's departure, a particularly brutal incident landed me in the hospital with broken ribs and a fractured left arm. On that day, it was my grandfather who rushed me to the hospital and later took over my legal custody after getting my father arrested. Those wounds twisted my perception of women. In my young mind, my mother's absence felt like a betrayal. I often wondered, if only she had taken me with her, perhaps I wouldn't have had to endure the void left by her love and the relentless onslaught of my father's aggression. To my dismay, she never even bothered to check if I was alive or not. This sense of abandonment deepened my resentment and suspicion towards women. As adolescence dawned, the lack of positive female figures in my life fueled my growing misogyny.

Then came the final blow. After serving his prison term, my father was released, only to meet a tragic end in a fatal car accident during my teenage years. His demise intensified my fury and cemented my negative beliefs about women, making forming relationships even more challenging.

Left to navigate life without parental guidance, my past traumas continued to haunt me. Due to the lack of a positive paternal influence and my deep-seated resentment toward women, I became a person I never aspired to be. My existence transformed into a battlefield of rage, bitterness, and distorted perceptions, all born from the scars of my family's tragedy."

My breath caught in my throat as I absorbed the weight of his words.

"My grandfather became my pillar of strength, the one who raised me, loved me, protected me, and bestowed upon me the affection I so deeply deserved. He stands as my sole family now, his unwavering support and unwavering love sustaining me through every trial." Ayank continued, his voice raw with emotion. "His dreams and sacrifices are the driving force in my life, a testament to the hope he harbours for my success, especially his dream of witnessing me being selected from RSS in the national football team."

His words echoed in the small space, and I felt the weight of his history press against my struggles.

“He saw the pain in my eyes, the void left by my mother’s absence. With wisdom born of experience, he recognized that channelling my grief and energy into the pursuit of this goal was about more than just football. It was a means of healing, a way to find purpose in the face of profound loss.” Ayank said, his voice carrying the weight of his loss.

“Every time I set foot on the field, I carried not only my aspirations but also the dreams my grandpa held dear. His dedication to my well-being and the sacrifices he had made for me served as both motivation and a poignant reminder of the love that had once embraced me. It was this love that fueled my determination to persevere, even when the challenges seemed insurmountable.”

His vulnerability lay bare, and Ayank’s story painted a poignant picture of loss, resilience, and the enduring love between a parent and child. His grandpa’s unwavering support, too, became a testament to the strength of family bonds.

Ayank’s voice wavered as he confessed, his eyes reflecting a complex blend of emotions—pain, regret, and an underlying fear of vulnerability. "And being near you, Sayami makes me kind of vulnerable. That sense of vulnerability led me to bring you to my grandfather’s place," he admitted his words carrying the weight of his struggle. "I fear that I might fail my grandpa by not being able to fulfil the dream he has for me. If word got out and he knew that I brought you to his place for a night, it could convey the wrong idea that I’m not committed to our shared dream. That’s why I urged you to keep it between us. And in my desperation to shield myself from that vulnerability, I ended up hurting you.”

His admission hung heavily in the air, each word echoing the battles he fought within himself.

Conflicting emotions swirled within me – anger, empathy, and confusion. The emotions he shared, the enigma that surrounded him, it all made me feel strangely weak. I struggled to maintain the shield around my heart, my anger fading as I saw the vulnerable soul beneath Ayank's confident facade.

"I messed up, okay?" he continued, his voice filled with regret. "I said things I shouldn't have, and I hurt you. I know I messed up, and I'm sorry."

"You can't just say hurtful things and then apologize, Ayank," I retorted. "It doesn't work like that."

He nodded, his expression pained. "I know, and I don't expect you to forgive me just like that. I just... I needed you to know that I'm sorry. I was stupid, and I regret it."

He looked at me, his eyes pleading for understanding. At that moment, I chose to let go of my anger, at least for now. I couldn't deny the connection I felt with him, the way he stirred something deep within me. I sighed, my resolve crumbling under the weight of his sincerity.

"I don't know if I can forgive you," I said, my voice softening.

"These past months, I've tried my best to keep my distance from you, to push away any thoughts or feelings," he said, his voice laden with sincerity. "But, Sayami, the truth is, being around you stirs up emotions I've kept buried for so long. There's something about you that draws me in and makes me feel things I thought I'd long forgotten. I believed that by being harsh or ignoring you, I could shut down these emotions. But it didn't work."

He moved nearer, his hand gently reaching for mine, intertwining our fingers together.

Ayank stood so close that I could feel his warm breath brushing against my lips, his presence enveloping me like an irresistible force. The proximity between us seemed to crackle with unspoken emotions, a magnetic pull that I struggled to resist. His eyes, intense and searching, held a mixture of desperation and longing, mirroring the conflict within my own heart.

In that intimate moment, the air between us grew charged with anticipation. His nearness stirred a whirlwind of feelings within me, a tumultuous blend of vulnerability and desire. I could sense the silent plea in his eyes, a plea that transcended words, asking for understanding, forgiveness, and perhaps a chance to bridge the gap that had kept us apart.

My breath caught in my throat, and for a fleeting second, I considered leaning in, succumbing to the magnetic pull drawing us together. But a war raged inside me—between the urge to yield to the emotions that swirled between us and the fear of being hurt once more. The conflict played out in the depths of my eyes, a silent struggle for control over my heart.

I was afraid of him. He had inflicted pain and humiliation upon me, yet, paradoxically, the enigmatic charm of the 'devil basher' had captivated me since the very first day I saw him. In that moment, part of me wanted to flee, but another part longed to stay, to immerse myself in the passion that seemed to surround him.

I held my ground, my eyes locked with his, my resolve wavering but unbroken. The electric tension between us hung in the air, a fragile thread that threatened to snap under the weight of our unspoken desires. At that moment, time seemed to stand still, as if the universe itself held its breath, waiting for the choice that would shape our destinies. In that moment, everything else faded away. The pain, the anger, the confusion—it all seemed insignificant compared to the connection we shared.

His hand, warm and tender, cupped my cheek, his touch gentle yet possessive. The world around us seemed to fade into the background as he slowly pulled me closer, closing the distance between our lips.

When his mouth met mine, it was like an explosion of emotions—a collision of desire, longing, and a profound connection that left us both breathless. His lips were soft yet demanding, tasting of an unspoken need that had been simmering beneath the surface. As our kiss deepened, every inch of my body came alive with a rush of electricity, setting my skin ablaze.

His fingers entwined in my hair, holding me close as if he never wanted to let go. I could feel the rapid beat of his heart echoing my own, the intensity of our shared passion becoming a palpable entity that enveloped us completely.

Time lost its meaning as we lost ourselves in each other. His tongue traced the seam of my lips, seeking entrance, and I willingly granted it, our mouths melding in a passionate dance. The taste of him, a heady mix of desire and something uniquely Ayank left me intoxicated.

A soft moan escaped my lips, lost in the warmth of our kiss. His hands, exploring the contours of my body, sent waves of pleasure through me, fueling the fire that raged between us. The world became a blur of sensations—the heat of his skin against mine, the urgency of his touch, and the intoxicating taste of his kiss.

Every touch, every sigh, every shared breath felt like an affirmation of the unspoken connection we had denied for so long. The kiss was a torrent of emotions, a culmination of longing and pent-up desire. At that moment, I abandoned myself to the intensity of our passion, allowing that kiss to drown out the world and the uncertainties that plagued my mind.

In that electrifying moment, I was lost in the intensity of Ayank's kiss, completely consumed by the passion that flared between us. Every fibre of my being longed to stay in that moment forever, wrapped in the warmth of his embrace.

But then, Eila's words reverberated in my mind like a sudden, chilling gust of wind. "Ayank is a womanizer," she had warned me, carrying me to the infirmary. Her cautionary tale had planted a seed of unease within me, growing stronger with each encounter with Ayank. This warning, now echoing in my thoughts for the second time since that night in the woods during the opening gala, bore a heavy weight. Doubt crept in, casting a shadow over the emotions that had entangled me with Ayank. I couldn't continue this cycle, ignoring the truths Eila knew about him. It was time to confront the reality of the man I was drawn to.

Instantaneously, the questions multiplied like wildfire. Was this just another cycle, another moment of weakness that would lead to more heartache? The words hung heavy in the air, casting a shadow over the emotions that had once been so intense. The battle between hope and scepticism raged within me, leaving me paralyzed in a state of emotional limbo. An uncomfortable feeling settled in the pit of my stomach, overshadowing the passion that had just enveloped us. With a sudden surge of resolve, I tore myself away from Ayank, my breaths coming in ragged gasps. His eyes, dark with desire and confusion, searched mine for answers.

"I can't," I whispered, my voice barely audible above the thumping of my heart. "Eila warned me to stay away from you, and I can't ignore her words."

Ayank's expression wavered between frustration and desperation. "Sayami, I don't know what she's told you, but please, let me explain."

But I couldn't bear to hear more. The turmoil inside me, torn between my growing feelings for Ayank and the cautionary words of my friend, left me in a state of emotional chaos. I turned away, my steps heavy with the weight of my indecision, and fled the room, leaving Ayank behind in the shadows.

Outside, the cool night air hit my face, grounding me in reality. As I walked away, I couldn't shake the memory of his passionate kiss, the taste of longing lingering on my lips. Yet, despite the undeniable chemistry between us, the warning bells continued to ring in my mind, leaving me torn between desire and self-preservation.

11

The End of Summer

As the summer break drew to a close, the memory of that passionate kiss I had shared with Ayank in the old changing room remained etched in my mind, haunting me persistently. Throughout the two months I spent at home, I found myself ensnared in a labyrinth of tumultuous emotions, the path ahead shrouded in uncertainty. The scorching sun outside mirrored the heat within and the memory of the kiss burned brightly in my mind. Amid family gatherings and lazy afternoons, my thoughts often drifted back to that stolen moment, leaving my heart in a constant state of unrest.

In the quiet hours of the night, I would replay the kiss in my mind, trying to decipher its meaning. Was it a fleeting desire or something deeper, something that demanded acknowledgement? Like relentless tides, doubts washed over me, each wave eroding my once-steadfast confidence. The conflicting emotions left me adrift, unsure of what to believe or how to proceed. It was a tumultuous inner battle, one that I knew I needed to confront when I returned to college.

One part of me longed for Ayank, enticed by the undeniable magnetic attraction we shared. The intensity of our connection had left an indelible mark on my heart, and I could not help but yearn for more. Yet, another part of me quivered with trepidation, bearing the scars of past hurts. The fear of being hurt again loomed like a shadow, casting doubt on the authenticity of Ayank's intentions. Strangely, he had not reached out to me after that passionate encounter, leaving me further in a sea of uncertainty.

Taani, my perennial problem-solver, and I reunited in our hometown after a year, during her visit back for the summer break. As I shared my dilemmas and concerns with her, she, too, suggested that Eila might genuinely aid in resolving my uncertainties. Now, an intense longing envelops me, urging me to confide in her, to reveal the intricate web of my emotions, in search of truth and seeking solace in her invaluable guidance.

The void left by Eila, my steadfast confidante, only deepened the turmoil within me. Our lives had been consumed by exams, and when she set off for her year-long student exchange program abroad, our interactions dwindled to a few sparse emails. Yet, the intricacy of my emotional dilemma far exceeded the confines of digital messages.

What did Eila know? Why did she say what she said in the infirmary? I had several questions and doubts rising in my mind to which I wanted answers. Her words lingered like a haunting mystery, and I felt a growing urgency to unravel the truth hidden beneath her warning. The unknowns stirred a tempest of emotions within me, and I knew that only by confronting Eila could I hope to find the clarity I so desperately sought.

Despite being a senior, Eila had always been my anchor from the very first day at RSS, the one I relied on for almost everything. Her absence left me adrift, wrestling with my inner demons in solitude. The distance only magnified the weight of my dilemma, and I longed for the day when I could reunite with her, face-to-face, and unravel the mysterious enigma named 'Ayank'. Until then, my heart remained heavy, burdened by unspoken words and unanswered questions.

"Where are you, Sayami? The movie's about to start. Hurry up!" My mom's voice broke through my maze of thoughts. I snapped back to reality, realizing I had to make popcorn. Absentmindedly, I had placed the corn kernels in the oven and lost myself in contemplation. Family movie night had become bittersweet as I prepared to return to college in just two days. The idea of returning held a mix of hope and apprehension. The only hope I had was in the conversations with Eila, which I hoped would aid in unravelling the complexities of my emotions. However, that possibility seemed distant, pending her return the following year. The impending end of summer not only signalled the close of a season but also the start of a profound journey I had to navigate alone. It was a trek into the challenges of the heart, a plunge into the depths of my feelings, and a quest for resolution that awaited me.

12

Group 6

As I scanned the class schedule pinned to the bulletin board, a sinking feeling settled in my stomach. I noticed that Ayank and I shared a biophysics class this term, and an unexpected wave of unease washed over me. Confronting him in every class suddenly seemed like an impending ordeal. Throughout the entire summer break, I eagerly but nervously anticipated returning to college, perhaps facing Ayank. However, now, the prospect of it all felt like a daunting task.

Eila had not yet returned and would be away for the entire year, leaving me stranded in uncertainty. How would I confront Ayank? What would I say if he approached me about abruptly ending the passionate moment we had shared in the old changing room? The questions swirled in my mind, leaving me apprehensive and lost in thought, dreading the inevitable confrontation.

The night before the first class had been restless, my mind swirling with anticipation and anxiety. As I made my way to the classroom the next day, my heart raced in my chest. The thought of facing Ayank, not knowing how I would react, filled me with a mix of confusion and fear.

Upon entering the classroom, I spotted Ayank, surrounded by his friends, engrossed in a conversation. My eyes met his briefly as

I moved through the crowd, but he quickly looked away, feigning indifference. Determined not to be affected, I ignored his glance and found a seat, trying my best to focus on the upcoming class.

The professor arrived, bringing a sense of order to the room. He began outlining the curriculum for the semester, explaining the various topics we would be covering. Just as the class settled into attention, the professor introduced a new twist to our learning experience.

"In our pursuit of enhancing team building skills and nurturing collaboration between seniors and juniors," the professor explained, his voice carrying authority, "I will be assigning practical assignments periodically throughout the term."

He continued, "Each group will be composed of two senior members and two junior members. The objective is to meld the seasoned expertise of seniors with the innovative perspectives of the juniors. Every Monday, you will receive a new practical assignment, which must be diligently worked on and submitted by the week's end, precisely on Friday. I must emphasize the importance of punctuality and dedication; failing to meet the deadline will adversely impact your grades."

His tone grew stern, underscoring the gravity of his words and the significance of the tasks at hand.

A sinking feeling overcame me as I grasped the implications. Fate, it seemed, had a rather ironic sense of humour. It was highly likely that Ayank and I would find ourselves in the same group. The prospect of working closely with him stirred a tumult of emotions within me - fear, curiosity, and a lingering sense of hurt that I'd been trying to bury. Ayank held an enigmatic pull over me, and it was difficult to imagine how I could simply ignore his presence. As the professor continued elaborating on the assignments, I braced myself for the challenges that lay ahead.

Our professor arranged two bowls, one labelled "Seniors" and the other "Juniors," each containing chits with our names. My heart thudded in my chest as I closed my eyes, silently praying not to be paired with Ayank. Fate, however, had different intentions.

"Mila, Sayami, Ryan, and Ayank will be in group 6," the professor declared, and my heart plummeted with apprehension. A silent scream echoed in my mind as I realized the challenge I was about to face.

As the professor announced the group, I caught Ayank's eye. He twisted in his seat, his gaze meeting mine, a devilish grin playing on his lips. An involuntary "ugh" slipped from my lips, capturing my frustration.

Determined not to work with Ayank, I decided to approach the professor after our class and request a group change. As the bell rang, signalling the end of the class, I hurried to catch up with the professor on his way to his office. Nervously, I asked, "Sir, is there any chance I could be moved to a different group?"

He looked at me with a stern expression. "The groups have been finalized, and no changes can be made unless there's a serious complaint, like harassment. However, filing such a complaint carries significant consequences. If proven true, it could lead to expulsion. Otherwise, group assignments are not subject to change."

Hearing the professor's words left me feeling utterly defeated. The prospect of working closely with Ayank was far from ideal, yet I couldn't bring myself to file a false complaint just to avoid his presence. My discomfort paled in comparison to the potential damage it could inflict on Ayank's reputation and his dreams of joining the national football team – aspirations that were intricately tied to his grandfather's hopes. Knowing the hardships he endured in his childhood, I couldn't bear the thought of being the cause of more problems in his life.

The weight of this realization held me in place, frozen in indecision. While I desperately wanted to escape the situation, I also couldn't bear the thought of causing harm to someone else, especially someone I cared for, albeit from a distance.

After a moment of internal struggle, I made a difficult decision. I chose to stay in the group, acknowledging the challenge but determined to complete the assignment professionally. The forced collaboration promised an uncertain journey, and I couldn't help but wonder how it would all unfold. I resolved to keep interactions with Ayank strictly related to the subject matter, avoiding any personal entanglements that could complicate the situation further. With a heavy heart, I resigned myself to the circumstances, hoping that focusing solely on the assignment would help me navigate the complexities of this unexpected partnership.

♡♡♡

13
A Cold Distance

I found Ayank standing alone in the hallway the next day. Mustering my courage, I approached him. "I'm not thrilled about working with you, but keeping this professional is the only way forward for both of us. We need some ground rules," I said firmly. "First, no humiliation. Second, we focus solely on the task at hand and give it our best. And third, we keep our private matters out of our discussions."

To my surprise, Ayank agreed without any protest. His usual smirk played on his lips, and in his eyes, I caught a glimpse of determination mixed with something elusive, something I couldn't quite put my finger on. His easy acceptance left me both relieved and intrigued, wondering what lay beneath his confident exterior and what this collaboration would entail.

Working together on the biophysics assignments for the term proved to be a challenging endeavour for Ayank and me. The unspoken words hung heavily in the air, the kiss in the old changing room a memory we both seemed determined to bury. Our interactions were infused with a peculiar mix of anger and undeniable attraction, creating an undercurrent of tension that crackled between us. Every conversation felt like a battlefield of witty retorts and subtle glances, a silent war of wills.

Yet, amidst our clashes, there was an unspoken understanding. We both recognized the importance of the task at hand and the gravity of the assignment that could affect not just our grades but also our future aspirations. This mutual awareness pushed us to put aside our personal differences, albeit temporarily, and focus on the task.

Every week, our group assignments loomed over us like a ticking time bomb, demanding collaboration and teamwork. We were experts at maintaining a cold distance, but beneath the surface, there was a magnetic pull neither of us could deny. The tension between us was palpable, a volatile blend of attraction and frustration.

Amid the pressure of deadlines and the complexities of our unspoken emotions, Ayank and I continued to work together on the biophysics assignments. Each week, as we laboured through the tasks, our stolen glances and wordless exchanges became the silent backdrop of our collaboration. It was as if the unresolved issues between us cast a shadow over our partnership, creating a tension that fueled both our attraction and the barriers we erected.

His eyes frequently sought mine, a magnetic pull drawing us closer, yet whenever our gazes met, he would hastily look away, as though retreating from something he wasn't ready to confront. Amid equations and research, our unspoken connection thrived, silently acknowledging the emotions we dared not voice. Our collaboration became a series of intense debates and heated discussions. Each idea I proposed was met with Ayank's challenging counterarguments, and vice versa. It was as if our disagreements fueled our determination to outdo each other, leading to an unexpected synergy. Yet, beneath the surface, the magnetic pull between us remained, an invisible force that both drew me closer and pushed me away, leaving me in a state of perpetual emotional conflict.

The questions lingered in my mind, though, like ghosts refusing to be banished. Was the kiss just a casual encounter for him, devoid of any real emotion? Did he feel nothing in that moment of passion? Eila's warnings echoed in my thoughts, creating a cloud of doubt that hung over Ayank's every action.

In those moments, I suppressed the urge to delve into the complexities of our connection. Instead, I channelled my energy into the academic tasks at hand, attempting to keep our interactions businesslike and devoid of any personal entanglements. The scholarship that I had earned through sheer hard work meant the world to me. It was my ticket to a better future, a chance to escape the limitations of my past. I couldn't afford to let emotions cloud my focus, no matter how much Ayank's presence unsettled me.

Meanwhile, our other group members, Mila and Ryan, a couple lost in their own world of romance, contributed little to the project. While we struggled through complex biophysics concepts and calculations, they often disappeared, indulging in their love-struck moments.

As frustrated as I was with Ayank, I couldn't help but be impressed by his intellect and dedication. In our disagreements, I saw a different side of him – a side that was passionate about the subject matter and driven to excel. And in those moments, despite our conflicts, a reluctant respect began to blossom between us.

Our group meetings, although tumultuous, were oddly productive. The clash of our minds generated innovative ideas, pushing the boundaries of our understanding. We might have been angry at each other, but that anger fueled a strange, electric energy that kept us engaged in the project.

Despite the turmoil, weeks turned into months, and somehow, we managed to complete our assignments on time. Every assignment we completed, to our surprise, was exceptional. Our combined efforts, despite the underlying tension, had resulted in a project that exceeded expectations. As we presented our findings to the class, there was a fleeting moment of shared pride between Ayank and me, a silent acknowledgement of the unexpected synergy that had emerged from our turbulent collaboration.

In those three months of working closely with Ayank, I found myself constantly wondering what was going on in his mind. His silent agreement to my terms and conditions was a stark departure from the Ayank I had known. There was a part of me that desperately wanted him to talk to me about the kiss, to address the storm of emotions that had been left unspoken between us. However, there was also a hesitant part within me that found an odd sense of relief in the quietude, a silence I had requested and one he had honoured thus far. Perhaps it was the doubts lingering in my mind that kept me from broaching the subject, but the uncertainty gnawed at me.

Despite the tumultuous history and the unresolved tension, Ayank surprised me. He kept his word by not humiliating me or making me uncomfortable in any way. He was surprisingly helpful and gentle, especially during our arguments. It was as if he was trying to bridge the gap between us, or perhaps he was dealing with his inner turmoil.

But the questions persisted. Why didn't he intervene when I ran away that night without a clarification? What did he truly feel? Did he experience the same intensity of emotions, or was I simply overthinking everything? The enigma that was Ayank seemed to grow more complex with every interaction, leaving me in a state of perpetual confusion, my heart torn between wanting answers and fearing the truths they might unveil.

14
Spilt Solvent

The sterile hum of the cryo-electron microscopy room enveloped us as we meticulously prepared the sample slide. The work was painstaking and time-consuming, so we had chosen to start early, seeking solitude in the hushed laboratory of the Central Instrumentation building. In the quiet of that room, there was only us. The tension between Ayank and me was tangible, the air crackling with unspoken words and emotions. His proximity, a mere breath away, as he stood slightly leaning on me from behind, stirred a whirlwind of conflicting sensations within me - a mix of attraction and discomfort warring for dominance.

I could feel the warmth of his body seeping through the thin barrier of personal space. The subtlest touch of his presence, an invisible force seemed to pull at my inhibitions, urging me to turn, to break the barriers, to surrender to the intense pull I felt toward him amidst the silence of the environment around us. The wave of desire coursed through my body, weakening my knees and sending a rush of heat that pooled in my core. In that charged moment, the silence of our surroundings amplified the intensity of our connection, creating an atmosphere thick with unspoken possibilities.

My focus wavered as my mind slipped into the realms of fantasy, an alternate universe where inhibitions faded, and desire reigned supreme. In this vivid daydream, Ayank's hands were strong yet tender as they lifted me effortlessly, placing me on the very countertop we had been working on. The world around us blurred into insignificance as he tore off my clothes, pushing my hair back and pulling it from behind, his lips intensely kissing my neck with soft bites. The soft moist lips passionately found their way back to mine, making me moan softly allowing our tongues to touch and caress each other's mouths. The intensity of the moment overwhelmed me, blurring the lines between reality and imagination.

Despite the unease, I resisted the magnetic pull, my eyes fixed on the task at hand. I refused to succumb to the temptation that hung between us, focusing intently on the delicate work before us, trying to drown out the alluring whispers of desire that seemed to dance around us. The sterile environment of the cryo-electron microscopy room became my sanctuary, shielding me from the intoxicating proximity of Ayank.

With every precise movement, I channelled my energy into the work, determined to maintain a professional demeanour despite the electric charge in the air. His closeness was a constant distraction, his body heat a reminder of the forbidden desires that threatened to consume us both. Yet, I pressed on, my hands steady, my focus unyielding, the intricate process of fixating the sample onto the slide grounding me amidst the chaos of my emotions. I couldn't afford to let my guard down, not now, not when the stakes were so high. The hum of the machinery became a rhythmic chant, guiding my hands and clearing my mind.

Despite the proximity, he remained silent, his eyes reflecting a storm of emotions I couldn't quite decipher. His usual expressiveness was replaced by a quiet distance, a subtle sadness clouding his gaze. The unbroken silence between us hung heavy with unspoken questions, each one adding layers to the complexity of our already tangled situation.

In that hushed atmosphere, the only sounds were the soft clicks of instruments and the rustle of lab coats. The clatter of the falling bottle shattered the fragile bubble of concentration that surrounded us. Startled, I turned to assess the situation, my eyes widening as I saw the spilt solvent seeping into the tiles. Ayank's sudden movement had caught me off guard, leaving me momentarily stunned.

Ayank's friends, their presence unexpected and unwelcome, now stared wide-eyed at the scene they had walked into. Ayank, his face flushed with anxiety, immediately shifted the blame to me. "Why can't you handle a simple bottle?" he spat, his tone laced with frustration. His words cut through the air like a sharp blade, accusing me of the accident, despite the truth being evident in the situation.

Confused and taken aback by his behaviour, I opened my mouth, desperate to defend myself, but the words caught in my throat, stifled by the lump of emotion that had formed suddenly. My stammer returned with a vengeance, my attempts to speak turning into a jumbled mess. "I... I... I did..." I managed to utter, but before I could complete my sentence, another blow came.

"The stutter queen is back, I see," Ayank sneered, his words cutting through me like a blade. "You can't even speak properly, and you expect to work with these delicate instruments and expensive chemicals? Ridiculous," he scoffed, his tone oozing disdain.

The lab technician, alerted by the commotion, hurried over. Ayank's accusations hung in the air, painting me as the culprit. I wanted desperately to explain, to clarify that it wasn't my fault, but the words eluded me. I felt a lump stuck in my throat, and my eyes stung with unshed tears. The lab technician, however, seemed uninterested in the truth. With a stern look, he asked me to leave the lab, his decision final and devoid of empathy.

Humiliated, I fled the lab, my footsteps echoing in the empty hallway. The weight of Ayank's false accusations and my inability to defend myself pressed down on me, suffocating me with a sense of injustice. I couldn't shake off the feeling of betrayal, wondering how Ayank, who I had tried to work with professionally, could turn on me so ruthlessly.

I didn't even wait to remove my lab attire before rushing out, tears streaming down my cheeks, my heart heavy with disillusionment. The trust I had tentatively placed in Ayank shattered at that moment, leaving behind a profound sense of hurt and betrayal.

Confusion and anger swirled inside me as I tried to comprehend Ayank's actions. Why had he pinned the blame on me for something I hadn't done? The pieces of the puzzle fell into place as I considered the situation. Ayank had panicked when his friends walked in, finding us in such close proximity. The fear of his reputation being tarnished might have driven him to deflect the blame onto me, ensuring that his image remained unscathed - a confession he had made previously.

The realization hit me like a tidal wave. It wasn't just about that moment; it was a pattern. He had manipulated situations before, whether it was when he took me to his grandpa's residence or during that impulsive kiss in the 'abandoned' changing room. Eila's warnings echoed in my mind, her words about Ayank being a womanizer haunting me. It wasn't just that; he was a misogynist too, a fact he had admitted, scarred by what his mother had done to him.

Was it prejudice, deep-rooted misogyny that made him recoil from any romantic entanglement, fearing it would mar his carefully crafted image? The bitter taste of betrayal settled on my tongue, and with each step I took away from the lab, I felt the weight of his actions pressing down on me, a harsh reminder of the reality of the person I thought I knew. I vowed that this time, I would not heed his explanations or extend forgiveness.

15

A Whisper of His Absence

I was engulfed in searing pain, consumed by agony, misery, and humiliation after the incident in the laboratory. The desire to hurt him back, to make him comprehend the depth of my suffering, burned within me. I refused to let Ayank continue to inflict pain on me, to apologize, and to expect everything to be mended. This time, I was determined to stand my ground and demand the respect and dignity I deserved.

The realization hit me like a cold shower when I realized spotting a small camera nestled inconspicuously in the corner of the lab. Suddenly, a glimmer of hope sparked within me. Perhaps, the footage could vindicate me, proving Ayank's lies. With newfound determination, I marched back to the Central Instrumentation building, my heart pounding with anticipation.

As the footage played on the screen, my eyes were glued to the monitor, hoping to see Ayank's deception unravel before me. However, luck was on his side; we were working in the one blind spot of the room. Disappointment settled like a heavy stone in my stomach, but I refused to be defeated.

In the dim glow of the library lights, I meticulously planned my strategy, a devious plot that would expose Ayank's lies and deceit. The biophysics class was approaching, and I intended to make him pay for his humiliation in the laboratory. I would demand he confess to his lies, threatening him with the illusion of the CCTV footage I didn't actually possess. The thought of him squirming in front of our classmates, facing the consequences of his actions, felt like a small victory.

The day of reckoning arrived, but Ayank was conspicuously absent from the classroom. I waited, my eyes darting to the door every few seconds, hoping to see him walk in with that usual swagger. But he never came. One day turned into two, then three, and eventually, four days passed without a trace of him.

Curiosity mingled with mild concern as I wondered why Ayank, the usually self-assured bad boy, was suddenly avoiding class. Every corner of the campus seemed to hold a whisper of his absence, a void where his confident presence used to be. The once-familiar places—a victory-filled stadium, bustling cafeteria, and lively campus corners—now felt strangely empty without him.

I found myself wandering through the campus, my eyes scanning the familiar haunts where Ayank used to roam. Each glance toward the door of the classroom held a flicker of hope, but he never appeared. The stadium, where he'd often display his athletic prowess, echoed with an eerie silence in his absence. Even the cafeteria, once a vibrant hub of activity, felt muted without his boisterous laughter and swagger.

The questions mounted in my mind like an insurmountable puzzle. Why was Ayank avoiding class? What could have made him retreat into the shadows? His absence seemed to add another layer of enigma to his already mysterious persona. I couldn't shake the feeling that there was more to this situation than met the eye, a secret beneath the surface that I was yet to uncover. As the days passed, the air crackled with unanswered questions, and Ayank's absence became an enigmatic void that begged to be filled with the truth.

Amid my contemplation, the professor announced yet another weekly assignment that needed completion before Friday. Panic gnawed at me; I had little time left and no partner to work with. Mila and Ryan remained indifferent, consumed by their realm of romance, and late-night escapades.

After battling with my wounded pride, I made a reluctant decision. Swallowing my anger and ego, I dialled Ayank's number, my fingers trembling slightly against the screen. The phone rang for what felt like an eternity before his voice crackled on the other end.

"Ayank," I began, my voice steadier than I expected, "we need to talk. I... I need your help with the assignment. I can't do it alone."

There was a moment of silence, his breathing audible through the line. Then, he spoke, his voice carrying a weight I hadn't heard before. "I can't meet you now, Sayami. Just handle the assignment on your own. I can't help you this time."

His abrupt dismissal left me both frustrated and puzzled. What was going on with him? Why was he acting this way? And why did he seem so distant? With the deadline looming, I had little time to dwell on Ayank's situation. Despite my burning questions, I had no choice but to hang up and complete the assignment and submit it on time, with or without his assistance.

16

A Part of My Life

The text notification buzzed on my phone, Ayank's name flashing on the screen. "Can you please come to meet me in the old changing room?" Irritation boiled within me. What more did he want after all the humiliation he had put me through? He had even left me to complete the group assignment alone. With a sharp tap of my fingers, I shot back a message, my anger evident in my words. "Why do you want to see me now? Haven't you done enough?"

His reply came swiftly, a request wrapped in an unusual politeness. "Please, just one last time."

My emotions were a chaotic blend of anger, hurt, and curiosity. Why had he been absent from class for the past week? Reluctantly, I agreed to meet him, the sense of foreboding growing with every step I took towards the old changing room. As I entered, Ayank was there, his presence filling the room, his eyes carrying a mix of regret and desperation. Something about that look seemed familiar, a facade I had seen before. But this time, I wasn't going to be fooled by it. I steeled myself, refusing to let his remorseful demeanour soften my resolve.

I held my ground, refusing to let his proximity affect me. "What do you want, Ayank?" I asked, my voice sharp with frustration.

He took a step closer, trying to hold my hand, but I instinctively moved back, out of his reach. "No," I said firmly, my eyes locking onto his. "You have a pattern, Ayank. And I won't fall for it again. What is it that you want to say?"

"My mom showed up," he said, the words laced with bitterness and disbelief. "She's dying from ALS, diagnosed a few years ago. Now, suddenly, she wants to be a part of my life."

A surge of empathy and anger coursed through me. I could sense his inner conflict, the battle between the longing for a mother's love and the resentment for her long absence.

Ayank's voice trembled with disbelief and anguish as he continued, "'How can she do that? Leaving me alone with an abusive father, only to show up when her own life is about to end. She suddenly remembers the son she left behind and wants to be a part of my life as if nothing ever happened." His words dripped with a mixture of disgust and pain, the bitter taste of abandonment and betrayal lingering in the air.

"I wasn't in the right state of mind," he confessed, his voice breaking slightly under the strain of his emotions.

He ran a hand through his hair, a gesture of frustration and helplessness. "I was angry," he repeated, his tone tinged with regret. "Angry at my mother for leaving me alone with an abusive father. Angry at the world for being so unfair. And when she suddenly reappeared, wanting to be a part of my life as if nothing had happened, all those emotions boiled over."

His hands clenched into fists, his knuckles turning white under the pressure of his emotions. "I didn't know how to handle it," he admitted, his voice barely audible, a mere whisper amid the charged atmosphere. "She appeared suddenly the night before the lab accident, triggering feelings of betrayal and abandonment once more. And when I was working with you, I felt I could not even pour my heart to you. I wanted to express myself, talk to you, but I felt emotionally paralyzed due to the childhood trauma inflicted by the woman who claims to be my mother. Lost in my thoughts and overwhelmed by emotions, I accidentally struck the bottle with my elbow, causing it to fall."

His eyes, usually guarded, now reflected the vulnerability he had long tried to conceal. "No matter how much I try to bring out the vulnerable side in me, the idea of being vulnerable engulfs me," he confessed, his voice wavering with the pain of admission. "When my friends unexpectedly arrived and found me alone with you, the fear of even being teased for any emotional attachment to you hurt my pride. I reacted by lashing out at you, trying to make it clear to them that there was nothing between us. I used you to prove a point, and for that, I deeply regret my actions."

At that moment, I once again saw Ayank not just as the enigmatic bad boy but as a wounded soul, grappling with the ghosts of his past. Yet, I couldn't let sympathy cloud my judgment. The pain in his eyes didn't justify his actions, and I couldn't allow myself to be swept away by his vulnerabilities, no matter how heartbreaking they were.

His vulnerability tugged at my heartstrings, urging me to soften, but I held my ground. Ayank's revelation about his mother's return might explain his erratic behaviour, but it didn't excuse the way he had treated me. No matter how much I felt for him, his presence around me had brought more pain than joy. It was time to let go of the fairytale fantasy I had been holding onto. I couldn't continue waiting for someone who was broken and a misogynist to change. Each time, I hoped for a meaningful shift, yet it remained an unending cycle—drawing close, inflicting pain, and then offering apologies. Recognizing the unbreakable pattern, I understood the need to liberate myself from this toxic cycle.

"No matter what your reasons are," I said, my voice unwavering despite the turmoil inside me, "I won't forgive you this time."

My words hung in the air, a final declaration of my wounded pride and the boundaries I had set to protect myself from further hurt. "Whenever you are around me, I feel uncomfortable, as if I'm on the edge of a precipice, unsure of what you will do or say to humiliate me. Being around you is just too unpredictable."

He nodded, his expression pained. "It's okay if you don't want to forgive me," he replied, his voice laced with regret. "I just thought you must know." His eyes pleaded for understanding. "I will switch groups, or better yet, take a medical absence from class if it makes you more comfortable.

"I glared at him, my resolve firm. "Do whatever you want, Ayank," I said, my tone bitter. "But it won't change how I feel about what you did."

Reluctantly, I agreed to his decision, my heart heavy with a mix of anger and disappointment.

ღღღ

17

The Looming Selection

The cafeteria buzzed with the rhythmic hum of conversation, the clinking of cutlery against plates, and the distant laughter of students enjoying their lunch break. Seated by the window, I gazed wistfully towards the sprawling football ground, a place that once echoed with Ayank's vibrant presence. The atmosphere was infused with a blend of nostalgia and concern as I pondered his prolonged absence.

The sunlight streamed through the large windows, casting a warm glow on the tables adorned with trays of half-eaten meals and steaming cups of coffee. Outside, the football ground lay quiet, a stark contrast to the lively days when Ayank's enthusiasm reverberated across the field. The memories of shared laughter and stolen glances lingered in the air, creating a bittersweet ambience.

As I stirred my coffee absentmindedly, the chatter around faded into the background, replaced by the echo of my thoughts. Two months had slipped away, each day leaving a void where Ayank's presence used to be. The nearing end of the semester cast a shadow over the routine, emphasizing the conspicuous absence of his familiar face in our common biophysics class. As promised, Ayank had deliberately distanced himself, keeping his word to spare me the discomfort his presence might bring.

The air was thick with speculation as rumours circulated about the reason for his extended medical leave. I sensed there was more to the story than what met the eye. He mentioned avoiding our common class to spare me discomfort, but his sudden absence from college has left me wondering about his reasons. The truth, like a subtle murmur in the wind, began to filter through the grapevine. Ayank, it seemed, was entangled in the intricate web of family issues, particularly revolving around his deserter mother.

The revelation added a layer of complexity to his absence. His promise to stay away from class, ostensibly to shield me from any potential discomfort, echoed in my mind. I found myself pondering the authenticity of his actions. Was Ayank's withdrawal a selfless act of consideration, a noble attempt to spare me from his troubles? Or, in the quiet corridors of his personal life, was he deeply immersed in the complexities of family dynamics and the struggles with his mother's decisions?

Yet, as the semester drew to a close, the impending Sports Academy selection day added a new layer of complexity to my emotions. Ayank, with his passion for football, had dreams that reached beyond the confines of our college campus. The desire to secure a spot on the national football team fueled his ambitions.

In Ayank's prolonged absence, the question loomed large: Would he show up to pursue his passion, defying the shadows that veiled his presence for the past two months? The prospect of his reappearance on the field stirred a mixture of hope and anxiety within me. The football ground, usually a place of jubilant cheers and spirited competition, now echoed with the uncertainty of Ayank's participation.

Amidst the eagerness to witness him chasing his football aspirations, there lingered a sense of longing. The absence of Ayank's presence, especially the familiarity in his eyes and the allure of his magnetic smiles became increasingly conspicuous as the significant day drew near. Despite the uncertainty around him, just one glance of him used to inject vibrant hues into the otherwise monotonous routine of my college days. The emptiness left by his absence became more palpable as the crucial day approached.

Yet, paradoxically, I found a strange tranquillity in the past two months—a reprieve from the potential emotional turmoil that seemed to accompany my connection with Ayank. The memories of constant humiliation, the repetitive cycle of apologies followed by promises to change, passionate moments intertwined with bouts of ghosting and reappearance—all these complexities had woven a toxic pattern into the fabric of our connection. In Ayank's absence, this toxic pattern seemed momentarily paused. The placidity derived from the absence of chaos and emotional turmoil created an unusual balance, albeit fragile.

With the looming selection day, I found myself standing on the precipice of conflicting emotions. The respite from the whirlwind of emotions was disrupted by the resurgence of concern about his well-being, the challenges he might be facing and the growing yearning to witness him pursue not just his dreams but also those intertwined with his grandfather's aspirations. The impending event became a pivotal moment, not only for him but also for the intricate tapestry of emotions that had woven themselves into the narrative of our shared experiences. In that moment, I couldn't help but wonder about the chapters yet to unfold in Ayank's story and how our paths might intersect once more.

18

In the Bleachers

The air crackled with excitement and tension as I made my way toward the football field, flanked by the eager crowd from the RSS. Today marked the culmination of aspirations for several talented players vying for coveted spots at the prestigious sports academy—an institution known for sculpting the future stars of the nation's football landscape.

Perched on the bleachers, my eyes scanned the field in anticipation, seeking out Ayank among the sea of players. And there he was, amidst the passionate chaos of the game, showcasing his prowess and determination. He moved across the field with an almost palpable energy, his every movement a testament to his skill and dedication.

As the match unfolded, Ayank's presence on the field was nothing short of awe-inspiring. He was a force to be reckoned with, a beacon of determination and skill that drew the attention of all who watched. His agility, finesse, and sheer passion for the game were unmistakable, leaving a lasting impression on the spectators, myself included.

Despite the gravity of the selection day, he seemed immersed in the game, pouring his heart and soul into every play. It was a sight to behold, a testament to his commitment and love for football. I found myself deeply engrossed in the match, silently cheering for him from the bleachers. Despite all the heartache he caused me, I couldn't help but feel an inexplicable surge of joy at witnessing his performance.

Seeing Ayank present on this momentous day filled me with a sense of relief and happiness. His absence during the past months had left a void, but now, watching him weave his magic on the field, I felt a sense of reassurance. His dedication and determination shone through, and I couldn't help but marvel at his resilience. As the game progressed, Ayank's exceptional performance painted a vivid picture of his potential. He stood out not just for his skills but for the fire that burned within him—an undeniable passion that set him apart from the rest. Amidst the thrill of the selection day, I felt a surge of pride knowing that he had shown up, ready to seize this opportunity to pave the way for his football dreams.

The euphoria of the selection match slowly dissipated, leaving behind a quiet hum of emotions swirling within me. Amidst the dispersing crowd, I caught sight of him approaching me in the bleachers, a mix of apprehension and vulnerability etched on his face.

As our eyes locked, a torrent of unspoken sentiments passed between us. Ayank's voice trembled with emotion as he began to speak, the weight of regret and longing palpable in his words. 'Sayami, I couldn't stay away today. I had to see you,' he confessed, his gaze searching mine for a hint of forgiveness.

My heart wavered, caught between the lingering hurt of the past and the sudden rush of emotions that Ayank's presence evoked within me. I stood, listening intently as he bared his soul, his words heavy with remorse and concealed pain.

'I lost my mother,' he revealed, his voice breaking with the weight of grief. "Despite it all, I remained by her side during her final moments. I was angry, wounded, but these past two months,

I couldn't bring myself to abandon her," he said, unveiling his vulnerability.

His revelation struck a chord within me, stirring a surge of empathy. I glimpsed beyond the surface, recognizing the intricate layers of his inner turmoil and the burden of his regrets and struggles.

"And as for my reputation," he confessed, his voice tinged with sincerity and vulnerability. "I've been labelled with many things, but meeting you changed me. I've made mistakes around college, earning the title of a 'bad boy' for reasons I regret. I've picked fights, hurt people, and misused privileges. But since that initiation night, since the moment I first laid eyes on you, everything changed. Your mere presence around me altered my entire world, shaking the very core of my existence. I haven't been with anyone else since then. I couldn't shake you from my thoughts. And before I realized it, I found myself falling in love with you, Sayami," he bared his soul, his eyes pleading for understanding.

Tears welled up in my eyes, a tumult of emotions swirling within me as Ayank's heartfelt words pierced through the walls I had built around my heart. His sincerity resonated with an honesty that echoed my sentiments.

I nodded, feeling the weight of my vulnerability, my voice barely a whisper as I responded, "I loved you too." In that moment, amidst the tears and the flood of emotions, I allowed myself to acknowledge the love that had taken root within me, despite the pain and the complexities of our journey.

Eyes moist with unshed tears, he took my hands in his, his touch seeking solace and redemption. "Please forgive me. I promise this will be the last time I hurt you," he implored, his eyes reflecting a profound longing and determination.

And then, with a tremor of emotion, he closed the distance between us, his lips meeting mine in a tender, heartfelt kiss.

It was a gentle touch, filled with a myriad of unsaid words—love, regret, and a silent promise for a new beginning. His kiss was a testament to the depth of his feelings, a bridge between our intertwined pasts and an uncertain yet hopeful future.

As our lips parted, the intensity of the moment lingered in the air, the weight of his confession echoing in the quietude around us. There was a vulnerability in his gaze, a silent acknowledgement of the risks taken and the emotions laid bare.

With a gentle squeeze of his hand, I met his gaze, offering a soft smile—a silent affirmation of the feelings stirring within me. It was a small gesture, yet it held the promise of forgiveness, understanding, and the possibility of healing.

The once bustling field, previously filled with football enthusiasts, now lay deserted. The weight of his confession lingered in the air, weaving our destinies together in a delicate tapestry of vulnerability and reconciliation.

Tears glistened in my eyes as I softly uttered, "I forgive you, Ayank. Let this be the last time you hurt me. I won't be able to bear anymore."

A subtle whisper within recognized the chance that this marked the juncture where the once "ruthless devil basher," heedless of anyone's emotions, including his own, evolved into "loving and empathetic" Ayank. It struck a deep chord within me, a poignant realization of his transformation.

19

The Newfound Happiness

In these past two weeks, Ayank and I have been inseparable. We've relished every moment together, making our college days feel like a whirlwind of happiness and togetherness.

I revelled in the newfound happiness that enveloped our college days. Walking hand in hand with Ayank through the corridors, the air felt lighter, as if the weight of the past had dissipated into the ether. The once-familiar surroundings of the campus now bore witness to our budding romance, painting each day with a newfound vibrancy.

Amidst the bustling college corridors and the hushed whispers of students attending lectures, Ayank and I clandestinely slipped away from the confines of our scheduled classes. With a shared smile and a knowing glance, we embarked on our own adventure, seeking solace in the quaint serenity of the woods around our college where he took me on the opening gala night about two years ago.

As we stealthily made our way to our rendezvous point, the air seemed electric with anticipation. The sun cast dappled shadows through the trees, creating a picturesque backdrop for our truancy. Nestled under the shade of an old oak tree, a secluded bench awaited our arrival.

There, surrounded by the gentle rustle of leaves and the distant hum of college activities, we found our private haven. Ayank's eyes sparkled with mischief as we settled in, relishing the stolen moments of freedom. Our hushed laughter filled the air, mixing with the soft melody of chirping birds.

The fervent embraces and passionate kisses we shared became a gateway to a heavenly realm each time he enveloped me in his arms. In those moments, the world faded away, and I found solace and bliss in the warmth of his embrace and the tenderness of his lips against mine. Each kiss felt like a symphony of emotions, transporting me to a place where time stood still, and only our love existed. It was in those intimate exchanges that I discovered an unparalleled sense of euphoria, a sensation akin to being cradled in the very essence of heaven itself.

In this hidden alcove, time seemed to stand still as we indulged in whispered conversations and shared glances that spoke volumes. The vibrant colours of blooming flowers provided a vivid contrast to the muted tones of our secret liaison, lending an air of enchantment to our clandestine meeting.

Our days were filled with shared laughter, lingering glances, and countless stolen moments. We spent afternoons in the college library, pouring over books while stealing secret smiles and whispered conversations. Ayank's passion for football was contagious, and we often found ourselves on the college field, him trying to teach me the finer points of the game amidst playful banter.

His presence brought a sense of calm and joy into my life. Our evenings were a blend of tranquillity and exhilaration. His genuine affection and efforts to make every moment special filled my heart with warmth. From taking leisurely walks around the campus, hand in hand, to losing track of time in deep conversations that ranged from our dreams to the mysteries of the universe, each conversation knitted our souls closer together.

Ayank's commitment to coaching football for the children at the local school every weekend was another secret he revealed. Seeing his love for the sport shine through as he patiently coached the kids filled my heart with admiration.

The newfound depth in our relationship was a testament to the bond we shared. Learning about Ayank's true self, and the vulnerabilities he had revealed, only deepened my affection for him. Eila's prior warnings seemed like a distant memory, eclipsed by the honesty, and love that Ayank had shown me.

Our time together was not just about grand gestures, but also about the small, intimate moments that made each day sparkle with newfound love and understanding. It was a journey I never anticipated, but one I embraced with every fibre of my being, cherishing every shared smile and tender touch.

20
Frostbeats

I entered the college field with Ayank, now transformed into the annual 'Frostbeats' winter music festival, where an exhilarating whirl of festive spirit and musical harmonies enveloped the atmosphere. 'Frostbeats' is a yearly celebration at RSS, where wintry melodies resonate throughout the night, melding harmoniously with the joyous revelry, colouring the chilly evening with a vibrant symphony of exultation and success. It's an electric ambience, alive with enchanting music, entwining cheerful celebrations and pulsating rhythms beneath the wintry sky.

When the long-awaited announcement finally arrived, Ayank's name echoed through the loudspeakers, triggering an explosive eruption of joy and exuberance from his friends. My heart swelled with pride and elation, mirroring the happiness that radiated from Ayank and his friends. In that fleeting moment, as the crowd cheered, the world seemed to come alive with an infectious energy, a perfect tableau of celebration and triumph.

As the music festival buzzed with excitement, Ayank's expression turned serious when he pulled me aside. "I have some news, Sayami," he began, his tone grave yet tinged with a hint of reassurance.

"What is it?" I asked, trying to mask my concern.

"I will be gone for the entire fourth year at the sports academy. I will only be back for exams," he explained, the weight of his words crashing into me like a sudden wave.

The festival's lively ambience seemed to dim as his words sank in. "You will be gone for a year?" I stammered, my heart sinking with each passing moment. The thought of Ayank's absence, someone who brought light to my days, felt overwhelming.

My heart sank, feeling a sudden emptiness, a void that wasn't there moments ago. The prospect of Ayank's absence, the one person who brought warmth to my life, was shattering. I struggled to hold back tears, the conflicting emotions raging within me.

"I promise, nothing will change between us," he reassured, attempting to offer solace in my spiralling emotions.

His assurances, though well-intended, couldn't dispel the heaviness in my heart. The reality of his impending absence weighed on me, and I found myself struggling to come to terms with the prospect of him being away for so long.

Amidst our emotional conversation, a drunk guy carelessly bumped into me, spilling his drink. I staggered, trying to maintain my balance, but before I knew it, I lost my footing and fell. Anger surged through Ayank, his protective instincts kicking in, ready to confront the guy who had pushed me. But, despite the rage, I intervened, pleading with Ayank to stop.

Reluctantly, he ceased his impending retaliation and instead proposed we head to his grandpa's residence for me to clean up, considering my dorm was closed for some installation until late midnight. It felt like a compassionate gesture amid the unsettling events, offering a sanctuary from the chaos of the evening. As we quietly walked towards his grandpa's place, my emotions remained raw, the vivid memories of the night's occurrences etched deeply in my mind.

Ayank's revelation about his impending absence lingered in the air, casting a shadow over our once vibrant celebration. As we walked towards his grandpa's residence, a heaviness hung between us, the weight of the news palpable in the chilly night air.

"I'm only halfway through college, Ayank," I murmured, my voice trembling slightly in the silence. "I don't know how I will get through the coming two years without you here."

Ayank's eyes held a blend of sorrow and determination. "I understand, Sayami. It's going to be tough for both of us. I can't imagine being away from you either."

"I thought things were finally falling into place," I sighed, halting our steps, my heart heavy with conflicting emotions. "This news, it's like everything's slipping away."

Ayank mirrored my pause and reached out, gently clasping my hand, a small gesture offering solace. "But I promise, Sayami, nothing will change between us. We will find ways to stay connected, to bridge the distance."

"I know," I whispered, a note of uncertainty in my voice. "But it won't be the same. I will miss you, Ayank. Your presence, your laughter... everything."

Ayank nodded solemnly. "I will miss you too, Sayami. More than words can express. But we will make it through this. I will visit whenever possible, and once I'm on the national team and you finish your graduation, I will take you with me."

My eyes shimmered with unshed tears. "I just don't want to lose you," I admitted softly.

"You won't," Ayank assured me, his voice gentle yet firm. "We will figure it out. I promise." He leaned in and kissed me tenderly.

The evening had been serene until the sky suddenly opened up, releasing a deluge of rain. The mountain rain, notorious for its unpredictability, caught us off guard, soaking us both.

Without hesitation, we hurried toward Ayank's grandpa's residence, racing against the downpour to seek shelter from the sudden storm.

21

Into His Embrace

I approached Ayank as we reached his grandpa's residence, feeling a bit uneasy about asking for a change of clothes. "Um, Ayank, do you have something I can change into?" I hesitantly inquired.

"Chill, I've got spare clothes stashed here for when my grandpa's away, and I crash here a couple of nights to take care of his plants and stuff," he replied casually, nodding. "Just hang on; I will grab something for you."

As he rummaged through his belongings, I stole a glance around the house, the familiar setting flooding my mind with memories. This was where I woke up once before, feeling out of sorts, after a crazy night at the gala. I was a bit out of it, and he had brought me here to ensure I was safe.

"Here, this should work," he said, breaking my reverie.

In his hands, he held an oversized black shirt, a gentle smile playing on his lips.

I offered a grateful smile and excused myself to the bathroom, grateful for a moment alone. I turned on the tap, letting the warm water wash away the stress of the evening. After a quick shower, I towel-dried my hair, feeling the damp strands cling to my skin.

Stepping out of the bathroom, I draped myself in the oversized black shirt that belonged to Ayank, the fabric embracing me in a cocoon and carrying a hint of his scent. Ayank's widened eyes met mine, appreciating the sight of his shirt on me, my damp hair forming a frame around my face. His captivated expression didn't escape my notice, and a sense of comfort settled within me as I caught his gaze. "You pull it off better than I do," he remarked. I found myself blushing.

Suddenly, with a loud clap of thunder, I jumped as the lights went out, leaving us in the dark. Ayank quickly grabbed his phone and used its flashlight to brighten the room. He then found some candles and a lighter from a nearby cabinet and expertly lit them up. Soon, the room was bathed in a soft, flickering glow as the candlelight danced across the walls, creating beautiful patterns and setting a magical atmosphere around us.

In the soft glow of candlelight, my eyes met Ayank's, and I found him chuckling and teasing me about my reaction to the thunder. "Scaredy-cat, huh?" he teased, and I retaliated with a playful pillow toss from the nearby bed. Swiftly grabbing the pillow, he tossed it back.

Caught up in laughter, I grabbed another pillow and flung it toward him. Soon, the room was filled with the joyous energy of a playful pillow fight, reminiscent of carefree childhood moments. Amidst the playful chaos, he managed to snatch the pillow from my grasp, but as I resisted, a loss of balance sent us both tumbling backwards onto the bed, him ending up inadvertently on top of me.

Chuckling at our sudden turn of events, our laughter gradually transformed into gentle, shared glances as we lay there, caught in a moment of closeness amidst the dimly lit room. In the ambient glow of the bedroom, the rain tapped a tranquil melody against the window, infusing the room with its soothing rhythm. Our eyes locked in an intimate embrace, I sensed a symphony of synchronized heartbeats resonating between us. With a tender and deliberate movement, he extended his hands towards mine, delicately intertwining our fingers in a silent pledge of eternal affection and devotion.

His touch was a caress of warmth as he gently brushed aside a stray lock of hair falling on my cheeks, leaving behind a trail of lingering sensations. I surrendered to the tenderness of his gesture, closing my eyes to get consumed in the moment. Cupping my face in his hands, his thumb traced the contours of my jawline, drawing me nearer, our breaths mingling in the crisp night air. A tender moment lingered, hesitating briefly before his lips met mine in a delicate, lingering kiss. It began as a feather-light touch, a shy exploration, before intensifying into a passionate embrace. His tongue traced the contours of my lips, seeking entrance. Yielding consent, our tongues wove together in a dance orchestrated by the rhythm of our hearts. I sought refuge in his hair, drawing him closer.

As the kiss deepened, an unspoken understanding passed between us, and with deliberate and unhurried movements, he began to undress me. He tenderly lifted my shirt, gently easing down the cups of my bra to liberate my breasts, his hold resonating with a palpable strength. Each motion was not merely a physical act but a revelation, peeling away layers not just of fabric but of vulnerability and raw emotion. As he leaned in, I noticed a scar adorning his shoulder, prompting a curious trail of my fingers, wondering if it bore witness to his athletic exploits on the fields. My hands navigated their way back, securing a fierce grip on his back, mirroring the intensity of passion pulsating through every fibre of my being.

As each layer of clothing fell away, it wasn't just our bodies that were revealed, but also the profound depths of our souls, laying bare our most intimate desires and vulnerabilities. I could feel my heart pounding fiercely within my chest, my cheeks flushing with a deep warmth. Immersed in his captivating scent and the seductive embrace, I yielded to the overpowering passion of the moment. As he bit my lips, his gentle caresses stirred longing sensations in my tender breasts, craving his touch. The kiss again escalated in urgency, his tongue intertwining with mine, igniting a passionate exchange. My body responded fervently; my nipples hardened as our bodies pressed together, my bare breasts meeting his chest. At that moment, I could distinctly feel the rhythm of his heart pounding in unison with mine. Our bodies merged in a slow, sensual dance, a union of flesh and spirit. It was a moment of profound intimacy, a celebration of the profound love we shared.

As I lay there, vulnerable and open, a gentle breeze danced through the curtains, carrying the soft fragrance of jasmine, cooling the heat that embraced my bare skin and the thumping pulse coursing through my veins. I felt a mixture of anxiety and excitement, an intriguing blend of emotions within me. Upon the silken sheets, his athletic presence cocooned my fragile frame, offering a haven of security and comfort. His gentle lips traced intricate paths across my body, emitting a warmth that sent delightful shivers coursing down my spine.

The facade of a devil basher, ruthless and heartless, he portrayed for a long time was convincing. He had a huge heart within him, so filled with warmth and love. And in this very moment, I relished on the fact that I was the only person on this planet who got to see what was underneath his hardened rude exterior. And when he finally let me see it, it was so damn beautiful, much more beautiful than the body he had.

His fingers caressed one nipple while occasionally giving it a gentle squeeze, while his mouth attended to the other, gratifying them with devoted attention. As his exploration continued downward, he traced a deliberate path with his kisses toward my navel, progressing inch by inch. Overwhelmed by mounting desire, my fingers instinctively tangled in his hair, guiding him as his lips traced the most intimate contours of my thighs, eliciting a surge of pleasurable anticipation. In a whirlwind of sensations, I couldn't suppress the involuntary moans escaping me and I arched myself toward him, a mixture of pleasure and the profound ache of desire for this enigmatic man who had captured my attention since our first encounter.

Suddenly, a jolt of electricity coursed through me as his lips reverently explored the holy grail of my being, tracing the revered curve of my temple. His skilful hands, with fingers and thumb adeptly exploring between my thighs, orchestrating a symphony of sensations—sucking, licking, and delivering tender nibbles that ignited a simmering desire, poised to erupt like a dormant volcano. Then, a sensation unlike any other as his thumb grazed a particularly sweet spot, causing my head to tilt back and my eyes to involuntarily roll. It was an unprecedented rush of sensation, shooting through every nerve in my body, in waves, I had never experienced before.

Overwhelmed by an intense surge of pleasure, an instinctual, raw groan burst forth from within me, echoing the waves of satisfaction coursing through my body. Every muscle in my thighs, belly, and bottom tensed and trembled in response to the overwhelming sensations, reacting as I contracted against his touch, feeling the effect of his fingers tracing my contours inside. I teetered on the edge, the escalating intensity felt both overwhelming and exhilarating. I felt myself oscillating on the edge, on the verge of being engulfed, shattered into fragments as the climax of sensation loomed near. The idea of him stopping triggered an instinctual impulse to cry out and beg for more. Simultaneously, I felt a desire to flee as it felt overwhelming, too much for me to take. Every cell in my body screamed with apprehension, fearing whether I could endure the impending intensity of what awaited me.

In the heat of the moment, I instead pulled him onto the bed and got on top, determined as ever. Smoothly, I undid his pants and slipped off his briefs. He grabbed my hair, holding it in place as I teasingly ran my hand along him before taking him in my mouth. His pleasure-filled noises filled the room as he savoured every moment, eyes closed. With a husky moan, I moved my mouth from base to tip, whispering, "Look at me." His taste lingered on my tongue, a salty tang. Caught up in the moment, I couldn't help but notice his strong, captivating presence that drew me in.

Swiftly, he guided me onto the bed, rolling me over as he firmly parted my buttocks and entered me from behind, delving deep within, evoking a blend of pleasure and a subtle twinge of discomfort that prompted a soft groan from my lips. Before I could fully collect myself, a curious expression crossed his face as he gently asked, "Is this your first time?" I nodded, confirming his query. With reassurance in his tone, he promised tenderness, initiating slow and deliberate movements. Softly checking in, he whispered, "Is it too much for you?" My whispered response of "no" conveyed a blend of sensations. "I will be gentle, my love. You are safe," he assured me. I trusted him, completely. Continuing our tender exchange, he maintained a deliberate rhythm, ensuring a delicate equilibrium between pleasure and my comfort.

The way he wore me on his skin and the way we fit, like we were made to be, felt like an ultimate connection. It was more than physical, it was beyond emotional, it was spiritual! There was nothing, absolutely nothing, that compared to the exquisite sensation of his rhythmic movements inside me. I felt closer to him than I ever had to anyone. Only If time would stop, I would live in this moment for eternity and beyond. I silently prayed that it would never be anything other than this.

He briefly paused, shifting me onto my back before commencing a sequence of rhythmic thrusts, passionately engaged between my legs. His ardour and arousal manifested in the intensity of his movements and the firm pressure of his hands against my soft breasts—alternating between gentle caresses and firm squeezes of my nipples. "Oh, darling," he gasped in response as I brushed my lips against his ear, teasingly licking and nipping with a gentle touch.

Unyielding in his rhythm, he persisted with deep and forceful thrusts, causing my bare breasts to bounce with each motion. The mirror strategically placed in front of the bed offered a complete view of the overwhelming passion enveloping us both. The initial sharp sting had now faded into a distant memory, completely overshadowed by the unparalleled pleasure of his rhythmic penetration.

The connection between us transcended mere words, each movement an intricate ballet of shared vulnerability and trust. The force of his thrusts against my hips urged me toward an inevitable release. The intensity of our silent conversations was intoxicating. The final thrusts ignited every inch of my skin with searing heat, sending electric sensations that pulsed through my body and soul. Sensations surged, reaching an apex where the intensity became overwhelming, compelling me to surrender control. It felt like an electric surge coursing through me, building to its pinnacle. "I can't hold on any longer," I cried out as I soared to the peak of climax. "Come with me!" he exclaimed.

In that very instance, as our orgasms burst forth together, I exploded into a million pieces, each spark merging with countless celestial stars into the cosmic expanse. And just for a moment, I transcended time and touched eternity. It made me ponder if I was alive, as my mind went blank, immersed in absolute nothingness—a sensation so captivating, akin to tasting a fragment of the unknown.

I opened my eyes to see the glistening beads of sweat on his forehead, and cold sweat dripping down my body - a testament to the intense and passionate lovemaking we shared. With a shared sigh, we both found fulfilment in the all-encompassing passion that consumed us tonight.

In the tranquil aftermath, solace found us in each other's arms, our breaths synchronizing into a shared rhythm. The world outside our sanctuary seemed distant and unimportant. Wrapped in an embrace, our bodies intertwined, our hearts melded into an unbreakable bond within the sanctuary of our love.

Gently, he shifted his position, moving from being above me to settling at my left side, his essence still lingering within me, a profound sense of satisfaction and the love we had shared tonight solidifying our connection. Holding me close, he tenderly kissed my lips, whispering affectionately, "I love you, Sayami." Nestling closer into his embrace, resting my head on his chest, I softly murmured back, "I love you too." His embrace offered comfort and warmth.

He held me snugly as weariness overtook me, a result of both the lively dancing at the music festival and the intimacy we had shared. Gradually, I drifted into a peaceful slumber, feeling content and joyful, cradled in the arms of a man I loved, and a person destined for greatness as a future football star.

22

Like Déjà Vu

As the morning light gently filtered through the curtains, I stirred from my slumber to the warmth of a tender kiss planted softly on my cheek, accompanied by a gentle murmur, "Good morning, my love." Slowly parting my eyelids, I found myself met with the endearing gaze of the man I cherished lying beside me. Inching closer, I closed the small gap between us, enveloping myself in his embrace while echoing, "Good morning to you too." Nestled snugly against each other, the comfort of our naked bodies provided a sense of cosiness and security that made me feel at ease. With a contented sigh, I drifted back into a light doze.

The tranquillity was interrupted by a familiar voice exclaiming, "Wake up, sleepyhead! I've made breakfast." It felt strangely familiar, like déjà vu. I blinked back to wakefulness, greeted by the sight of him holding a tray laden with a variety of delectable treats he had meticulously prepared. The aroma of freshly ground coffee lingered in the air, accompanied by the inviting scent of toast adorned with sides of strawberry jam and butter. Alongside, a plate of perfectly poached eggs sat next to a vase of freshly picked jasmine, enhancing the ambience. Placing the tray on the bed, he leaned in for a sweet morning kiss, which I eagerly reciprocated, the remnants of our passionate night still lingering in my heart. Blushing yet content, I found myself lost in the moment.

"Why don't you have something to eat and then head back to the dorm to get ready for classes today? I will stay and clean up the kitchen mess, then meet you at the college later," he suggested warmly, interrupting my reverie. With a mouthful of toast and a grateful smile, I nodded in agreement. However, before I could fully indulge, an incoming message illuminated my phone screen. It was Eila, finally back after a year-long exchange program at a university abroad. Excitement surged through me at the prospect of reuniting with her. Ayank noticed the sparkle in my eyes and inquired about the sudden joy.

"Eila is finally back!" I exclaimed with pure elation, my excitement evident. His response was somewhat subdued, lacking enthusiasm. Sensing a ripple of unease, I gently probed, "What's wrong? Is something bothering you?" He brushed it off with a vague assurance, "No, nothing. We're getting late for class. Why don't you freshen up and head back to the dorm to get ready?" His attempt to redirect the conversation was evident as he took hold of my hands.

Finishing my breakfast, I bid him a quick goodbye at the residence gate, feeling a mix of excitement and anticipation, eager to reunite with Eila after a year-long separation. With my mind buzzing with thoughts of our impending meeting, I hurried off towards the dormitory, eager to catch up and share the stories of our time apart.

♡♡♡

23

Irony Wasn't Lost on Me

As I swung open my dormitory door, a surge of joy rushed through me at the sight of Eila standing there, her face radiant with excitement. With uncontainable enthusiasm, she exclaimed, "Hi! Where were you? I arrived around 4 AM this morning and didn't find you in your room, so I took a nap. I've missed you! There's so much to catch up on." I rushed towards her, enveloping her in a tight embrace. "I missed you too! I've been waiting the whole year to share everything," I exclaimed, feeling overwhelmed with emotions at our long-awaited reunion.

We settled on my bed, eager to delve into the tales of our respective journeys during the past year. Eila kicked off the conversation, regaling me with stories of her adventures abroad, her fascinating experiences, and the diverse cultures she encountered. With each tale, her eyes sparkled with excitement, and I couldn't help but be captivated by her animated storytelling.

It was finally my moment to share, and I couldn't contain my excitement. The very first words that escaped my lips were, "This morning, I was at Ayank's place. We spent the night together," I confessed, feeling a rush of happiness that tinted my cheeks with a blush. Eila seemed surprised by my revelation, her reaction a blend of astonishment and disbelief as she stuttered, "What? When did this happen, and how?"

Gathering my thoughts, I began to narrate the tumultuous emotional journey I experienced with Ayank. "It all started last year, right before the final exams, when he kissed me. He apologized for the previous embarrassments he had caused, but then things became distant between us over the summer break. I wasn't entirely sure if Ayank would change. I wanted to discuss it with you, but you were away too," I explained, recalling the past events.

"After returning from the summer break, fate seemed to intervene, placing us together in the same biophysics class and even in the same assignment group. Unfortunately, Ayank reverted to his previous behaviour, humiliating me in front of his friends and the lab technician during our assignment work," I continued, a tinge of hurt evident in my voice.

"I was deeply hurt and determined not to forgive him. Consequently, he took a medical leave to avoid the class entirely so that I would feel comfortable in his absence. We went our separate ways, and it wasn't until nearly a couple of months later that he approached me to apologize and clarify his behaviour," I recounted, revisiting the challenging moments with Ayank. "He opened up about his past, revealing how his toxic conduct stemmed from a childhood marred by an abusive father and an absent mother who unexpectedly reappeared after years of abandonment, only to tragically pass away," I explained, unveiling the intricate layers of Ayank's troubled history.

"Recently, Ayank tried out for selection in the sports academy, and he got in. The results were announced yesterday during the frostbeats. After his sincere apology and promise to change, he proposed to me on the selection day," I revealed, a blend of emotions in my voice. "I said yes and decided to give him a chance because, despite everything, I have strong feelings for him. Since then, he has made me nothing but happy. He's a changed man now, and I love him."

Eila appeared stunned and bewildered by my confessions, her mouth agape trying to articulate a response, but only air escaped. Observing her reaction, I was taken aback. "Say something, please. I can see you're trying to process that someone like Ayank could have this side to him in reality," I urged, sensing her disbelief and astonishment. "But trust me, he's not how he appears to everyone. He has a vulnerable, loving, and caring side that many people don't get to see."

"I had a feeling something like this would happen. There's something important you really need to know," Eila said with concern. "I feel terrible that I was away for so long; otherwise, I would have told you this much earlier, before Ayank tried to get close to you."

"What do you mean?" My excitement swiftly turned into concern at her words.

"Sayami, Ayank isn't who he pretends to be. He's not the good, caring, vulnerable guy you think he is just because he shared some sob story. Something dreadful happened to me when we were freshmen," Eila disclosed with a tone of concern and urgency.

"What are you trying to tell me?" I retorted sharply, my irritation turning into a sudden outburst. My blood seemed to pulse through every vessel, as if on the verge of exploding.

"I told you he's not a good person and warned you to stay away from him. Don't you remember when I took you to the infirmary?" Eila's voice trembled with the weight of her words. "It's because he drugged me the night of our gala. At first, he was friendly, we danced, and then he shared his story about his abusive father and absent mother. Later, he spiked my drink, took advantage of my intoxicated state, and filmed me at his grandpa's place. The next morning, when I confronted him, he threatened to share the content he created with everyone at the RSS, making my life a nightmare."

"When I sought justice and reported the incident to the director, his grandpa's influence shielded him. The entire administration, from the highest levels downwards, seemed to be against me. Instead of addressing the issue, I was pressured to drop the complaint to prevent any defamation of Ayank. It felt like his influential status as a football player, RSS's eagerness for a spot on the national team, and his grandpa's financial power over our college overshadowed the need to address the injustice I had faced," she explained, her voice laden with frustration and pain. "If I persisted, I would've been expelled on charges of adultery and misconduct. I had to complete my degree and move forward, so I had no choice but to bury the matter and continue as if nothing had happened."

"Since that night, I've carried silent pain and resentment toward Ayank, hoping to prevent any other girl from falling into his trap," Eila confessed, her voice heavy with the burden of her secret.

"He is my classmate, but you probably never noticed me talking to him. I don't even like seeing him," she added with deep contempt. "He's a manipulative bastard. If the devil existed and had a name, it would be Ayank."

"'To prove what I'm saying, the next morning I took pictures of the marks I had on my body, and I could show you,' Eila said as she searched through her phone, opening the images and displaying them to me.

I stared at the images, witnessing the bruising and forceful marks, unable to utter a single word, feeling a mixture of betrayal and foolishness. A heavy stone seemed lodged in my throat, the pain coursing through my body. My heart weighed heavy, and my soul screamed for salvation. The love I had held dear was shattered, nothing but a facade of lies and manipulation. I struggled to contain my tears, but they broke through. I couldn't bear to stay in the room for another moment. I ran. I didn't know where, but I ran, trying to escape from the reality I had just faced.

Tears streamed down my face as I sprinted down the dormitory hallway. Feeling suffocated, as though I couldn't breathe, I ran desperately, searching for some semblance of air. My legs led me toward the field, as if drawn by an unseen force. Upon reaching the desolate football field, I collapsed at the exact spot where Ayank had made me cry that fateful initiation night. The irony wasn't lost on me; he was Ayank. It was foolish of me to believe he could be anything else.

My mind wrestled with conflicting emotions, torn between hurt, anger, and a heart-wrenching realization. The weight of this understanding was so overwhelming that I felt an immense pain capable of consuming me entirely. It was a torment so profound that it seemed as though I might not survive it. The intensity of the emotions threatened to engulf me, leaving me feeling utterly shattered and lost.

24

Like an Incessant Swarm of Bees

Tears streaming down my face, I sat hunched over on the desolate football ground. Suddenly, a chill gripped my arms as someone's cold hand lifted me from the ground. "What's wrong? Why are you crying?" Ayank's voice cut through my despair as I looked up, startled by his unexpected presence.

Confusion and hurt enveloped me. He was supposed to head to college after cleaning up the kitchen mess, yet here he was. His presence felt like just another lie. Deception was his habit. I didn't want to hear any more falsehoods from him. Struggling to break free, I was determined to escape his deceitful facade.

"Just go, Ayank. I don't want to talk to you," I spoke through clenched teeth, my voice filled with frustration and pain. Pushing his hands away from mine, I felt a surge of anger and a torrent of tears streaming down my cheeks. Fuming with a mix of emotions, I briskly began walking toward the cafeteria, hoping against hope that, given his and his grandpa's respected reputation, he would let me go, sparing me from any public confrontation or potential lies about his past misdeeds.

"Just tell me what happened. Did I hurt you? Did I do anything? Just let me know," Ayank's voice trailed after me as he attempted to reach out. I halted abruptly, feeling the tension coil in my shoulders as I pivoted to face him.

"You said you'd be at college after cleaning the kitchen. But where were you? Let me guess - here, finding me in this mess." I gestured sarcastically around the desolate football ground, my voice trembling with hurt and frustration. "And what about Eila? I know what happened in your freshman year. Don't even try to deny it."

Shock painted his features, rendering him speechless. He stood there, unable to muster a response as his silence spoke volumes. With a heavy heart, I turned away, tears streaming down my face, and hurried toward the cafeteria, trying to escape the tumultuous emotions that engulfed me.

"Sayami, please wait, let me explain!" Ayank's desperate plea echoed behind me, but I couldn't bear to listen. My shattered heart couldn't handle any more explanations, especially from him, the source of my pain and confusion.

"What is there to explain, Ayank?" I choked out, my pace quickening, my voice a mix of hurt and anger. "I feel so foolish. This goes beyond mere lies or humiliations. You're not just deceitful, you're a truly malicious person. That sob story you fed me was just a ploy to manipulate me, wasn't it? And what you did with Eila is beyond atrocious, unveiling the depths of your character to me."

"Perhaps, with me, you had it easy. Maybe Eila wasn't as naive as I was to trust you," I continued, bitterness coating my words. Rage seethed within me, rising to a fever pitch, while an unrelenting torrent of tears flowed down my face, and my heart felt as though it could burst from the overwhelming pain at any moment. The sting of realization pierced deeper; it wasn't just my trust he had exploited, but Eila's as well, and potentially countless others. The pain of being deceived and used felt intensified, a shared betrayal that highlighted the extent of Ayank's manipulative and heartless nature.

I pressed on, my steps determined, a desperate attempt to create distance from the whirlwind of emotions engulfing me. The pain of his deceit resonated through every word I uttered, entwined with the frustration of recurrent disappointment.

This time, it wasn't merely about the fleeting instances of humiliation he had caused me before. It cut deeper—it involved an inhumane act, a crime that shook me to my core. It was something irredeemable and utterly unforgivable. The mere thought of his presence made my stomach churn with disgust. I walked faster, my resolve to escape his proximity growing stronger with every step.

Ayank took a step closer, his eyes pleading, "Please, just hear me out. I didn't lie to you this time. I promise."

His persistent pursuit only fueled my anguish and repulsion. I wanted to escape the turmoil, to find solace away from his haunting presence. But his persistent shadow loomed, a reminder of the pain and revulsion I wished to leave behind.

I shook my head, my emotions bubbling over.

"Sayami, I can explain everything. Please, give me a chance to clarify."

"Explain? How can you explain away the hurt you've caused? How could you do this to me?" I scoffed bitterly, my emotions entangled in a web of betrayal and anguish. "Okay, just tell me one thing — you never took Eila to your grandpa's residence on the night of the opening gala in your freshman year, the same way you took me?"

He paused for a moment, his response carrying a weight of guilt and evasion. "I was a different person back then. I made mistakes, terrible ones. But that's not who I am now. I've changed, Sayami. Please, believe me."

I shook my head, the pain in my chest deepening. "I can't do this, Ayank. I trusted you, and you shattered it into a million pieces. I told you it would be the last time you hurt me."

He took a step closer, his voice desperate, "Please, at least just hear me out before taking any decision. I care about you, and I truly love you Sayami. I'd never want to hurt you intentionally."

The rawness of my emotions overwhelmed me, and I blinked back tears. "But you have not only hurt me but enjoyed publicly humiliating me! And we both know that. And I can't do this," I whispered brokenly, walking away, feeling Ayank's gaze linger on me, filled with regret and longing.

The bustling cafeteria seemed a blur as I hurried, Ayank's persistent attempts at explanation buzzing around me like an incessant swarm of bees. Lost in my own tumultuous emotions and tear-blinded, I failed to notice the person in my path, colliding accidentally with him as I rushed towards the exit.

The impact sent scalding hot coffee cascading over me, searing my skin with pain that paled in comparison to the raging inferno within. Before I could register the agony, Ayank, in an abrupt and violent frenzy, gripped the guy by his collar, ruthlessly shaking and throwing punches in a fit of rage.

I gasped, a mixture of shock and horror flooding my senses. Desperate to halt the escalating violence, I attempted to intervene, but my efforts were futile. The commotion drew a crowd, their curious gazes fixed on the chaotic scene unfolding before them.

"This is who you truly are, Ayank! Not the facade you showed me in the past few weeks. You're not even worthy of being called human – you're a monster!" My voice trembled with a mix of hurt and disgust. "I feel sick at the thought of ever trusting you. I never want to see your face again. Just get lost."

With those words echoing in the chaos, I turned and ran as fast as my feet could carry me, desperate to escape the turmoil and find solace in the solitude of my dorm room. The betrayal I felt cut deeper than ever, leaving scars that seemed irreparable. The realization that the person I thought I knew was a far cry from reality left me shattered, questioning my judgment and the sincerity of those around me.

25
The Last Vestige

I rushed out from the infirmary, a storm of anxiety and confusion swirling within me. Despite Ayank being away at the sports academy for almost a month and my efforts to dodge his persistent attempts to contact me, his shadow seemed to loom over me, disrupting my quest for a normal student life at RSS. Panicked and unsure, I hurried back to the dormitory, my mind reeling with uncertainty.

Seeking solace, I hurried to Eila's room. Gasping and visibly distressed, she was taken aback as soon as I blurted, "I'm six weeks pregnant."

"Wait, what!" she exclaimed in disbelief.

"Yes, I went to the infirmary, and the tests indicated I'm six weeks along," I confirmed, my worry and panic evident.

Eila looked shocked, her concern etched across her face. "What are you going to do now? You're not planning to keep it, are you?"

Emotions surged within me, a complex mix of love, pain, and confusion. Despite unearthing Ayank's true character, a part of me clung to the love I thought we shared. The yearning for the person he pretended to be clashed painfully with the reality of who he truly was. The internal conflict tore at my heart, but I couldn't discard the profound connection tied to the night we shared our love. The thought of relinquishing the last vestige of Ayank—the love I held for him and the love we made that night—felt excruciating.

After a moment of contemplation, I replied with a quiver in my voice, "I've decided to keep my baby. It's not their fault that things didn't go as they were supposed to."

Eila sighed, her concern evident as she expressed her worries. "Are you certain about this? Please, think about the implications. Remember, it's Ayank's child—someone who doesn't care for anyone but himself, is involved in questionable actions and is a rapist. Are you prepared to raise the child of someone like him? Moreover, you still have nearly two years of your graduation left. How will you manage your studies, and your future career, with a baby? And considering the potential scandal it could cause in RSS, it might endanger the successful career you rightfully deserve."

Eila's words, though undeniably true, pierced deep into my heart, evoking a pain that brought tears welling up in my eyes. "I'm not dwelling on it more than I did before. I never considered these consequences when I allowed myself to believe in false hopes—hoping for change, love, or the belief that he wouldn't just use me. Sadly, that warning of yours, Eila, proved to be true," I lamented, feeling a blend of stupidity, disgust, and pain swirling within me. The bitter realization of falling for those false promises despite warnings left me feeling deeply regretful and hurt. Nevertheless, I held firm in my decision. "But now, when another life, an innocent being, is at stake, I cannot turn away. I've made my choice—I'm keeping this baby, regardless of any potential scandal."

"What about Ayank? Are you planning to tell him about this child?" she asked, her tone laced with concern and contempt.

"No way! Sure, biologically this might be his child, but I won't allow my child to grow up to be like him," I remarked with a bitter tone.

“He follows a pattern - hurts, apologizes, I forgive, and then it all repeats. But this time, what he has done goes beyond forgiveness. It is heinous and unforgivable. I feel disgusted at believing that he could be a good person or he could really love me. Even if he knew about the child, it wouldn’t affect him. He is heartless, remember? His concern only revolves around himself," I continued, a trace of scorn tainting my words.

"Okay, if that’s your decision. But be prepared; this might bring trouble," Eila cautioned.

"Yes, you’re right. I'm deeply concerned about how to break this news to my family. They will see me as a disgrace. Despite their efforts and financial struggles, all they wanted was for me to succeed and build a better future. Knowing what I did instead will break their hearts and disgrace me. But at the same time I can’t allow an innocent life to be denied existence because of my past foolish decisions," I confessed, a blend of disdain and self-contempt colouring my words.

The weight of my decisions, the fear of family repercussions, and the resolve to protect the life growing inside me mingled into a storm of emotions, leaving me grappling with the daunting path ahead.

26

Intricate and Multifaceted

"I think I might have a solution," Eila approached me, interrupting my intense focus on the impending assignment deadline. "About what?" I inquired, slightly puzzled by her sudden intrusion.

"Look, you can have your baby, pursue your career, and prevent problems at home, all without risking a scandal at RSS that could harm your future," she explained, her face bright with determination. Intrigued, I paused my work, stood up, and crossed my arms, inviting her to continue.

"What would that be?" I inquired, curiosity and anticipation filling my voice as I looked up at Eila, eager to hear her idea.

"Your pregnancy is becoming noticeable, and before it triggers rumours leading to potential scandal and further complicates things when you reveal the situation at home, I spoke to my aunt. She's open to offering assistance," she explained, her tone serious and weighted with concern as she brought up the sensitive issue.

"What exactly are you suggesting?" I pressed, urgency lacing my voice, seeking clarity on her proposal.

"So, you know my family history—my parents and my one-year-old sister died in a car crash when I was five. I was the only survivor, raised by my aunt who's my sole family now. I confided in her after what Ayank did to me, and she's aware of what happened with you too. She's determined to assist you. She understands your connection to your baby and wants to help you keep it without causing turmoil at college or home," I explained, trying to grapple with the weight of her proposition.

"Could you be more direct, Eila? I'm struggling to understand," I requested, feeling a whirlwind of confusion and disbelief.

"Alright, here it is. My aunt runs an orphanage in my hometown, and we can organize a fake adoption," Eila disclosed, her voice unwavering as she delved into the plan.

"You could take a medical leave from college and reside at my aunt's place until the baby is born," she began, her words measured and deliberate. "Then, my aunt would arrange for the baby to be 'put up for adoption' on paper, while she will actually care for the child. During your time at college, you will ask your mother to find a suitable partner for you, mentioning feelings of loneliness and a desire to settle down. Post-graduation, once you're married, you can persuade your husband to adopt the child, completing the faux adoption process."

She paused, letting the weight of her proposal linger in the air. "This way, you can have your baby and a life partner. Moreover, before the adoption is finalized, you could discreetly visit your child without anyone ever knowing the truth," she explained, her plan intricate and multifaceted, layered with complexity, underscoring the gravity of the decision she was suggesting.

"What!" I exclaimed in a mix of shock and growing irritation, feeling overwhelmed by the complexity and ethical dilemmas of her proposal.

"No, I can't agree to this! I won't bear the weight of deceiving my parents or manipulating someone into adopting a child born from a reckless college situation. It's unthinkable! How could you even consider such a thing? I'm already shattered and laden with pain; I can't bear any more. It would haunt me forever," I expressed, my distress palpable in my voice as I grappled with the implications of her plan.

27

Despite My Deceit

I sat by the window in the café, the last traces of daylight painted the room in soft hues of orange and pink. Absently, I traced patterns on the surface of my now-empty coffee cup, my mind a whirlwind of conflicting thoughts and emotions. The person I once was seemed a lifetime away—a studious introvert with aspirations, now replaced by someone unrecognizable, hollow, and filled with a sense of loss. Love had reshaped me into this unfamiliar figure, leaving behind a trail of anger and emptiness—a price for the choices I had made.

During my spring break of the final year, I met Nilay after my mother introduced us. He happened to be the son of a family friend. Gradually, over a few months, our friendship blossomed. Despite my withdrawn nature, enveloped in my thoughts and choosing my words sparingly, Nilay found something remarkably captivating about me. His subtle yet genuine affection gradually evolved into a marriage proposal.

As I awaited Nilay's arrival, I grappled with the weight of the deceit that tangled around me. Eila's counsel, though a lifeline when given, now felt like a noose tightening with each passing moment. Deceiving my family and Nilay, who genuinely cared for me, tore at my conscience. With our wedding on the horizon, the turmoil within intensified. The decision regarding the orphanage had left me emotionally and physically shattered. And the urge to confide in Ayank tugged at my emotions, but I resisted, knowing his true nature.

Nilay's arrival snapped me out of my reverie. "Where are you lost? I've been calling out, but you didn't hear," he asked, his voice laced with concern and a hint of a smile.

"I needed to talk to you about something important," I began, the gravity of my confession weighing on me. "It's significant, and if you choose not to marry me after this, I will understand," I prefaced, observing the worry etch itself onto Nilay's face.

"What's wrong?" he inquired, leaning closer, his expression a mix of worry and curiosity.

"When I was in college, I got involved with someone who manipulated me, someone I thought was good. I became pregnant with his child," I disclosed, peeling back the layers to reveal the child's true origins. "Eila introduced me to her aunt's orphanage, where I gave birth to my son. Her aunt would care for him until I completed my graduation and found a job," I explained, tears welling in my eyes. "I could not even tell my family. Eila suggested I agree to marry someone and then fake-adopt my own baby. I continued with you to regain custody of my son, who remains in the orphanage. Besides, I thought marriage would provide him with a father he would otherwise never have."

Nilay seemed visibly taken aback, processing the revelations I had just disclosed. "I've made foolish decisions I deeply regret, but this—I couldn't continue," I confessed, feeling the weight of guilt bearing down on me. "You've been kind and supportive, loving me despite my deceit, but I couldn't keep this from you. I know I've hurt you deeply, and I understand if you no longer wish to marry me."

As Nilay processed the weighty confession, a heavy silence hung between us. The café seemed to quiet down, the soft murmurs of distant conversations fading into the background. His eyes reflected a storm of emotions—surprise, disappointment, and a hint of hurt—mingled with a deep sense of concern for me.

"Sayami, this is a lot to take in," Nilay finally spoke, his voice calm but tinged with the complexity of his thoughts. "I wish you had told me earlier, but I appreciate your honesty now."

"I couldn't find the courage, Nilay. I feared losing a friend like you," I admitted, my voice trembling slightly. "But I couldn't bear the thought of hiding it from you any longer, especially when we're about to start a life together."

Nilay reached out and gently grasped my hand, his touch offering a sense of reassurance amidst the turmoil. "I understand. But why did you keep this from me for so long?"

"It's a part of my past that I'm not proud of," I confessed, a sense of shame colouring my words. "I was trapped in a situation that spun out of control, and I felt suffocated by the choices I made. His gaze softened with empathy. "I wish you had confided in me earlier. We could have faced this together."

"I know, and I regret not trusting you enough," I replied, feeling the weight of missed opportunities for honesty between us. "I care about you, Sayami and I love you. And if this is what you need to find closure and happiness, I'll stand by you. We will adopt him after we get married," Nilay affirmed his unwavering support offering a glimmer of hope amidst the shadows.

Exhaling deeply, a mix of relief and guilt washed over me. I was grateful for his compassion and understanding amidst my tangled web of deceit.

ღღღ

28

An announcement

As I carefully nestled my son into his crib, soothing him into a restful sleep, a gentle chime from my laptop broke the tranquillity of the room. I had been anticipating an email—details of an experiment for tomorrow that I needed to study. Hastily, I glanced at the screen, only to be taken aback by an unexpected sight: an announcement about the upcoming alumni meet at RSS, just a month away!

Memories flooded back in a torrential rush. It had been a while since my last conversation with Eila, our lives drifting apart amid her bustling work life in the States and the ever-widening gap between our time zones. Despite our attempts to stay connected, our communication had become scarce, a mere thread tethering us together.

The inner turmoil struck me like a bolt of lightning. The announcement stirred a maelstrom of conflicting emotions within me. A compelling question loomed large: should I go?

Part of me was drawn irresistibly toward the idea—to encounter Ayank once more, to confront the past, and maybe, just maybe, to finally hear the version of the story I had never allowed him to tell. The mere possibility of seeing Ayank sparked a flicker of hope within me—the part that eternally wished for the good in him, the part that yearned for the man I fell deeply for, and the man I once believed he could have been. But in reality, that was a facade, a fragile wish tethered to a reality that had shattered long ago. It was a wish that lingered, perpetually distant, and forever out of reach. The truth was stark—what Ayank and I had shared was a product of manipulation, a fleeting mirage that dissolved upon closer inspection.

Ayank's mysterious and alluring darkness, the very magnetism that once enchanted me, now cast a shadow over my thoughts. It was a harsh reminder that falling for the allure of the devil only brings pain, tears, and a hollow loneliness. Every time my mind dared to hope, my heart would shatter into a million fragments, reminding me of the stark truth, of what he had done to Eila. I grappled with the raw contrast between what I had dreamt and the harsh reality I was forced to accept. Our relationship, I realized, was a product of his manipulation, a ruse that burnt my heart and led me astray. The hope to bridge the gap, to rewrite our story, seemed nothing but a naive fantasy, miles away from the bitter truth.

I couldn't evade the reality. The longing to uncover the truth from Ayank was intertwined with the pain of knowing it might forever remain a fantasy—a mere illusion I had clung to, harbouring an unending hope against the odds. The prospect of attending the alumni meet stood as a crossroads between confronting the past and allowing it to fade away into oblivion.

Three years had passed since the day I confronted the truth, since the storm of turmoil and problems crashed down upon me, leaving me to navigate the tempest alone. After just a fleeting couple of months, Ayank's silence spoke volumes. It was a deafening testament that the bond I thought we shared was merely a trophy—a conquest he swiftly moved on from. His lack of longing for me, the absence of any attempt to reach out, punctuated the truth—I was just a passing chapter in his story, while he was the harbinger of an enduring storm in mine.

Despite my relentless dedication to burying emotions beneath the weight of my career pursuits, working tirelessly in the research and development department of a prestigious pharmaceutical company, the echoes of the past reverberated persistently within me. Emotions had become a luxury I couldn't afford, except for the love I held for my son, my sole motivation for providing him with everything I possibly could. However, a nagging question loomed large in my mind - would Ayank even grace the alumni meet with his presence? Or had our shared history faded into distant memories for him, overshadowed by his ascent to football stardom? The uncertainty clawed at my thoughts. Would his words, if uttered, carry the sting of deception or simply indifference?

In my swirling uncertainties and mounting apprehensions, a faint glimmer of hope stubbornly lingered—an enduring yearning for closure. It was the chilling prospect that Ayank might make an appearance at the upcoming alumni meet, potentially offering that elusive final conversation—a chance to bury the haunting spectres of the past and draw the veil over a chapter that had cast its long, dark shadow over my life. Perhaps I could summon enough courage to extinguish the hope that flickered within me, crushing it to satisfy my intense curiosity about his undisclosed narrative.

Deep down, I knew, like many emotional choices that had led me astray before, this encounter might very well lead to yet another mistake. Yet, the longing for closure, the desperate yearning for resolution, remained steadfast, refusing to be silenced despite the risks.

29

Completion of a Circle

As I approached the convention centre, a rush of nostalgia engulfed me, triggered by the mesmerizing decorations and the faint sound of music emanating from within. The sight of the grand hall brought back vivid memories of my freshman year, a time when Ayank's mischievousness had left me with a blend of fury and irritation, courtesy of the humiliating dance he coaxed me into performing on my very first night at RSS.

It was a moment I desperately wanted to avoid, yearning to dodge any direct encounter with him. Fate, however, had its course charted out for us, and we ended up meeting that night, dancing amidst the crowd. It was an evening etched in my memory, the night Ayank revealed fragments of his tumultuous childhood, leading us to his cherished spot in the woods.

Now, as I approached the entrance, my heart fluttered rapidly within my chest. Despite the hurt and the feeling of foolishness that lingered, my emotions took precedence over logic. I yearned to find Ayank, to possibly have a final conversation. I understood that this might be the last opportunity to meet him. In my mind's eye, I already visualized the closure this conversation could bring.

Lost in my reminiscences, I entered the convention centre and spotted Eila standing within a circle of her batchmates, engaged in cheerful conversation. I hastened towards her, and as soon as she caught sight of me, she threw herself at me, enveloping me in a tight, cheerful hug.

"Sayami! It's been almost two years! I've missed seeing you around. You look stunning in that silk drape," Eila exclaimed, her eyes brimming with joy. "Come on, let's grab a drink and catch up on our lives. I've got so much to share with you!"

Despite her enthusiasm, I was in a rush, so I gently shook off her hand and inquired urgently, "Eila, have you happened to see Ayank around?"

As Eila heard my question, a furrow appeared on her brow, her eyes clouded with concern. "Why? What's happened?" Her voice held a tremor of worry, sensing the urgency in my tone. "I need to find him. I need to talk to him!" My desperation was palpable, an urgency that couldn't be contained. "I don't think this is a good idea, Sayami," she cautioned.

"Just tell me if you've seen Ayank or not?" I pressed on, the insistence in my voice betraying my anxious state.

"I don't know. I haven't seen him around. I'm not sure if he's here or not," she replied uncertainly.

"I will go find out," I declared, determination guiding my steps as I hurried away. My heart beat fervently in my chest, convinced that he was around somewhere. There was an unshakable sense that I couldn't disregard, the anticipation of seeing him after three long years pulsating through me.

I scoured every corner of the campus. However, an inner voice persistently nudged me toward the football field - his sacred sanctuary and the place where our paths first crossed, fatefully urging me toward the completion of a circle. As my legs carried me swiftly toward the field, a few meters ahead, I noticed a figure seated by the bleachers. I paused, straining to discern the silhouette in the dim glow of the stadium lights. It was Ayank, just as I had anticipated.

The sight of him after all this time caused my heart to race uncontrollably, its frantic rhythm echoing in my ears. Part of me urged to turn away, knowing that confronting him had always resulted in pain. But another part of me, like a moth to a flame, was inexplicably drawn to him. I couldn't resist and hurried toward him, calling out, "Ayank!"

He seemed lost in his thoughts until my voice disrupted the reverie. His startled gaze met mine, "Sayami!" he exclaimed, rising from his seat and descending the bleachers. With every step, his pace quickened, closing the distance between us on the open field.

Amidst the rush of emotions flooding through me, a jumble of conflicting feelings surged as he stood there, looking into my eyes with a mix of surprise and familiarity. "Sayami," he exclaimed, his voice tinged with both astonishment and something I couldn't quite grasp.

Unable to contain the whirlpool of emotions any longer, I reached out and embraced him tightly. Yet, as my mind collided with the harsh reality of what he had done to both Eila and me, I recoiled from the embrace. Tears welled up in my eyes, a floodgate of emotions threatening to overflow. The dream I had nurtured in my heart for so long collided mercilessly with the stark truth—the truth I desperately needed to hear.

"I need to talk to you. I need closure," I pleaded, my voice breaking. "These years have been nothing but misery. I need the truth. Just tell me that you manipulated me, that you used me for your own gain. It will be easier for me to move on knowing that. For so long, a part of me held onto hope, hoping against hope that maybe, just maybe, there was something real between us. That what we had was genuine and what you did to Eila was a mistake that could be erased. But I know it's not true. Tell me you're just a terrible person who manipulated and used me. Please, just this once, tell me the truth," I sobbed uncontrollably as I spoke, my heart wrenching with each word.

"I didn't do anything with Eila. I've been trying to tell you for so long, but when I found out you're married and have a kid, I assumed the truth no longer means anything to you," his words struck me like a bolt. "How did you find out about my baby and the marriage?" I couldn't contain my curiosity, as Eila was the only person who knew about my son and my marriage to Nilay—it was her suggestion.

"After I left for the sports academy, I started experiencing symptoms like palpitations and dizziness while playing football. I ignored them until one day during the final national team selection match, I collapsed. Rushed to the hospital, I was diagnosed with Wolff-Parkinson-White syndrome, a heart condition that, while not immediately life-threatening, could become dangerous without proper treatment. It shattered my dream of being on the national team. I needed specialized treatment called cardiac ablation, which wasn't available here, so I had to travel to the States. Meanwhile, my grandpa also passed away. I've spent the past two years there, grappling with my condition and trying to escape from the emotional trauma I experienced here. Perhaps it's my karma for all the bad things I did. But despite my past, I didn't do anything with Eila," he explained.

I was left silent and taken aback by his revelation. "I'm sorry, Ayank, for what you went through," I offered sincerely.

"Instead, Eila actually came and apologized to me for everything she put me through and became a true friend, supporting me through every emotional struggle. She was there for me during everything, especially when my grandpa passed away and I felt like I had no one left, no one I could call family," he added with a solemn tone.

Stunned and utterly confounded, I struggled to find words. "And today, I came hoping to maybe see you, maybe talk to you, but Eila insisted I should stay away as the loud music could be harmful to my recovering heart," Ayank explained, holding my hand, his eyes heavy with emotions.

His words lingered, enveloping me in a cloud of confusion. Why would Eila apologize to Ayank? What is there that I don't know? And why did Eila conceal her closeness to Ayank when she was the one who had shared the pain he caused her, asking me to steer clear of him? Everything felt like a puzzle with missing pieces. The revelation spun my thoughts into a whirlwind of emotions and unanswered questions. The contradiction between her past words and her actions now left me disoriented, lost in the maze of conflicting truths.

"I need to tell you something, Ayank," I began hesitantly, feeling the weight of the unspoken truth. "There's something you should know." Every lie had to unravel for the truth to surface.

"My son, his name is Ayaansh. He's ours," I stated. "When you left for the sports academy, I found out I was pregnant. I chose to keep it a secret, hurt and furious. Eila suggested that I give birth at her aunt's orphanage and leave our son there until I finished my graduation and secured a job. It was a secret I held close, hidden from my family and everyone else.

My emotions were tangled in resentment towards you, driving me to work tirelessly day and night to complete my studies and secure a decent job. All this while, I grappled with everything on my own, without any support, and I had no one to turn to for guidance except Eila. So, I trusted her and followed almost every suggestion she offered." I confessed, a trace of disappointment and pain seeping into my voice.

"In the meantime, I was on the brink of marrying Nilay, arranged by my mother. When I revealed the truth to him, he was willing to marry me and adopt our son. But I couldn't go through with that marriage. Instead, I chose to be a single mother," I explained, each word carrying the weight of years of concealed truth and the emotional turmoil it brought.

I stood there, watching Ayank's immediate reaction, the emotions visibly waging war within him. His face contorted in a mix of pain, anger, and sorrow, an unspoken turmoil that raged behind his eyes. It was a tempest of emotions, a storm that no words could quell. Silence hung between us, heavy and suffocating, a palpable tension that seemed to engulf the entire space.

"Sayami, I can't believe that you kept this from me," Ayank finally managed to utter, his voice trembling, mirroring the storm of emotions raging within him. "How could you not tell me about our son? How could you keep him away from me all this time?" Ayank's words were laden with intense emotions, a mixture of disbelief, hurt, and a desperate longing for the child he never knew existed.

“But I understand. I was not an ideal person. You would have wanted to not give our son a father like me. I understand your situation. I left you all alone to deal with the storm, and now I can't stand here and complain. I do not blame you, but it is my own deeds that brought me this consequence," he continued, his voice thick with emotion.

His hurt pierced me deeply. "I'm so sorry Ayank," I whispered, the weight of my confession weighing heavily on my conscience.

"I should have been there for you," he muttered, his voice laced with self-blame and regret. "I trusted Eila, and she kept us apart as she promised on that gala night."

His words hit me like a brick, a sudden revelation that shook the foundation of my understanding. "What do you mean?" I asked, confusion clouding my mind, desperate for the truth.

But Ayank's shoulders slumped further in defeat, and it was evident that the wounds inflicted by the past were deeper than I had ever imagined. He turned away, leaving me engulfed in a torrent of guilt and an urgent need for clarity.

"Tell me, Ayank! What do you mean?" Confusion engulfed me, and the urgency in my voice was unmistakable. I reached out, holding Ayank's shoulders, shaking him in my desperation for answers. "What did Eila say? What did she do?" Every word was an echo of my escalating confusion and the overwhelming need for clarity.

Amid the confusion and desperate plea for answers from Ayank, suddenly, a searing, excruciating pain erupted within my chest, a sharp, intense agony that seemed to pierce my very being. Clutching my left side, I staggered, struggling to maintain balance, but the searing pain was overpowering. My legs gave way beneath me, and I crumbled to the ground, gasping for air.

As I stumbled, Ayank reacted swiftly, catching me before I hit the ground. He caught me in his arms as I fell, his eyes wide with shock and horror. I felt a flood of unbearable pain engulfing my chest, making every breath a battle. Each inhalation became an ordeal, causing stabbing, knife-like sensations that shot through me. Blood pooled in my mouth, and a violent fit of coughing erupted, the metallic taste of blood staining my lips.

I knew, in that terrifying moment, that I had been shot. Ayank held me tightly, his face a portrait of panic and anguish as he fervently attempted to control the bleeding. Frantically calling for help, his words spilled out in urgency, a desperate plea for assistance. The world around me began to blur, sounds dissipating into a distant echo, while darkness slowly encroached on the edges of my vision.

I fought to stay conscious, my gaze locked with Ayank's tear-filled eyes, but the pain was overwhelming. With a final effort, I tried to speak, to reassure him, but the words wouldn't come out. The world spun, and everything faded into an eerie blackness as I slipped away, unconsciousness claiming me.

30

A selfish desire to live on

As I stirred, the faint murmur of hospital machinery greeted my senses. Blinking slowly, I saw a familiar figure standing at the foot of the bed. Ayank. His eyes, filled with concern, met mine as I tried to sit up.

"Sayami, thank goodness you're awake," Ayank said, his voice a mix of relief and worry.

Trying to ask about Ayaansh, I attempted to speak, but a sharp pain shot through my chest.

"He's fine, Sayami. He's safe. He's in the hospital's playroom with other kids," Ayank reassured me, understanding my unspoken worry. He reached into his pocket and retrieved an envelope, extending it toward me. "Eila left this for you."

I nodded, accepting the letter with a blend of anticipation and a tinge of apprehension, pondering what Eila might have conveyed in writing that she couldn't express in person. I carefully tore it open, unfolding the pages to read her words.

Dear Sayami,

It is difficult to put into words the torrent of emotions I feel as I write this letter to you. There is an ache in my heart, a deep regret that weighs heavily on my soul. I need to confess, to unburden myself of the deceit and the wrongs I have committed against you.

All this time, I have hidden truths not to hurt you, but from an unreciprocated love and an obsession that clouded my judgment. I have deceived, lied, and twisted circumstances, all in a futile effort to distance you from Ayank—someone I loved profoundly but could never have.

The truth is, everything I told you about what happened between Ayank and me was a fabrication, a twisted web of lies spun out of desperation and unrequited love. That night at the gala, Ayank did nothing wrong. I approached him, and during our conversation, I shared the tragic story of my parents' crash, hoping to capture his attention and appeal to his empathy. He reciprocated by trusting me and revealed his own painful experiences with an abusive father and a deserter mother. He was a gentleman, helping me when I pretended to be drunk. I took this as an opportunity to further get closer to him.

After purposefully spilling the drink, I requested a change of clothes, prompting him to take me to his grandpa's place for that purpose. However, upon arrival and finding ourselves alone, I bravely confessed my feelings to him, and he, quite honestly, rejected me. He said that he saw me as a friend, nothing more. His rejection pierced my heart like a dagger, causing immense pain.

I was engulfed in a tempest of emotions—anger, hurt, and the burning desire for retribution. In my frenzied state, I acted impulsively. I tore at my clothes, and inflicted wounds upon myself, capturing made-up evidence, an elaborate ruse to fabricate a tale of assault. I could not bear the thought of Ayank finding love elsewhere while I silently endured rejection.

As Ayank pleaded, attempting to dissuade me from this path of destruction, my heart hardened with vengeance. My mind echoed with a singular, bitter resolve: if he would not be mine, then no one would have him. I threatened him of spreading rumours, warning that any attempt at a relationship with anyone would result in the annihilation of his reputation, his dream for the national football team — his very essence. He never crossed any line, Sayami. It was my actions that led to the chaos.

But then you entered our lives and in the wake of my torment, I observed the budding connection between you and Ayank with a turbulent heart. I knew his tendencies, his subtle gestures, and the flicker of interest he held in you. It drove a wedge deep within me, stoking the fires of jealousy and resentment.

I confess I endeavoured to keep Ayank at a distance from you. The thought of witnessing his affection for someone else, especially you, my friend, ached in a way I can scarcely articulate. It clouded my judgment, leading me down a path of more deceit and manipulation.

During my year-long internship, the thought of you getting closer to Ayank plagued my thoughts incessantly. Yet, deep down, I knew Ayank would not do anything to jeopardize his and his grandpa's cherished dream of making it to the national football team. Nevertheless, upon returning and discovering the events of the Frostbeats night, a sense of desperate panic overwhelmed me.

In a state of panic and desperation to regain control, I poisoned your perception of Ayank by falsely accusing him of assault and presenting manufactured evidence of self-inflicted harm. I was aware that this lie would undoubtedly fracture the delicate bond between you and Ayank, especially with his imminent departure to the sports academy.

But the revelation of your pregnancy shattered what little remained of my already fractured heart. Despite this, I could not let go.

I could not bear the thought of Ayank's devotion swaying toward you and the child. I took deliberate actions to orchestrate events, including the fake adoption, to ensure your marriage to someone else, shielding Ayank from the truth about his imminent fatherhood. In doing so, I not only lied to you but also deceived my aunt, manipulating her into supporting plans she would otherwise have never supported.

However, after I graduated, fate took an unexpected turn that initially seemed advantageous to me. Upon learning of Ayank's illness and his grandfather's passing, a different side of me surfaced—an intense pang of guilt mixed with a genuine desire to be close to him and perhaps win his affection. I saw an opportunity to stand by his side, convincing myself that his emotional vulnerability would pave the way for forgiveness. So, I took a job in the States just to be near him, hoping to win him back through sincere apologies and by being there for him.

I must confess that my intentions were clouded by selfishness. I viewed this as a chance to reconcile with Ayank, taking advantage of his vulnerability. I was also successful in convincing him of how happy you were in your marriage and with a son, so he would not attempt to re-enter your life. At the same time, I anticipated your resentment, assuming that you would distance yourself from him, harbouring hatred for what you believed he did to me. This secured my closeness with him.

However, the announcement of the alumni meet shook the delicate balance I was building my life upon. Despite my resistance, Ayank did not stop from coming, and I had to attend to prevent him from meeting you. But fate seemed to have entangled our destinies once again, and you suddenly appeared at the alumni meet, desperately searching for Ayank to speak with him. I realized that if he discovered the truth about his son, nothing would prevent him from reuniting with you, and I would lose him forever. The thought was unbearable, and in a fit of anger, I impulsively decided to end your life by shooting you. In a state of panic, I fled, determined to get as far away as possible. Yet, consumed by anger, I couldn't depart without confirming that you were truly gone for good.

At the hospital, I overheard Ayank speaking with the doctor about the seriousness of your injury caused by the bullet, the damage to your left lung demanding an immediate transplant for your survival. Witnessing Ayank holding Ayaansh, tears streaming down his face in a way that surpassed any emotion he might have felt for me, stirred a tumultuous mix of feelings within me. At that moment, it became painfully evident that my aspirations for a life with Ayank were futile—they were never meant to come true.

In a sudden epiphany, I recognized the extent of my misguided actions. I had become caught in a web of selfishness and irrationality by keeping a father away from his son and obstructing the path of love towards its rightful destination. The enormity of my deeds dawned on me, and in an attempt to rectify even a fraction of the damage I had caused, I made a drastic decision.

At the hospital, where you may be reading this, I inflicted a gunshot wound upon myself and left behind a direct donor form. I specifically indicated that my lung tissue should go to you. As twisted as it might seem, it was my way of ensuring a lingering presence in Ayank's life—every breath you inhale with my lung would serve as a reminder of my existence. It is a selfish desire to live on, to remain close to him in a way I have always longed for, even if it's through the intricacies of our tangled breaths of love.

I realize this does not justify my actions or make me a good friend or lover. I cannot undo the damage I have caused. But it was my final attempt to remove myself from your path and offer you a chance at the love you deserve. Please know that my intentions, however flawed, were rooted in a desire for something I could never truly possess—Ayank's love.

In the labyrinth of my misguided actions, I failed to see the wider repercussions, the irreparable damage inflicted on both of you. I stand here now, burdened by the weight of my misdeeds, yearning for redemption, but aware that forgiveness may forever elude me.

I reveal these truths without seeking absolution, fully aware of the depth of my wrongdoings. My sole wish is that time may ease the wounds I have inflicted and that someday, amid the aftermath of my actions, both of you might discover solace and healing.

With heartfelt regrets,
Eila

As I read, Ayank stood there, watching me read, his presence silent support in this moment of upheaval and revelation.

The letter was a testament to her apologies, detailing the truth she had hidden from me. With every word, a sense of betrayal and confusion engulfed me. She had woven a complex tale of deception and misguided intentions, explaining her actions and revealing secrets that shattered my already fractured reality.

Tears welled in my eyes as I read her heartfelt expressions of regret, apology, and the reasons behind her actions. Mixed emotions of anger, disbelief, and a strange understanding washed over me. It was a letter that seemed to explain so much yet left even more questions lingering in my mind.

In the grip of painkillers or amidst the swirl of thoughts in my mind, I found myself in relentless contemplation. As I delved into my thoughts, I could not evade pondering: what could have been the alternate course of my life if I hadn't crossed paths with Eila on that first day at RSS? How might the narrative have been different with Ayank? The thought journey led me to deeply contemplate the immense impact a friend can wield in shaping life's trajectory.

It required enduring years of bitter experiences and immense pain for me to grasp the dual nature of a friend—a fusion of positivity through unwavering support and negative effects through misunderstandings or misguided actions. Their positive influence brings joy, but their negative traits often pose challenges, revealing the intricate and layered complexity of human relationships.

And then, there's love—an emotion wielding an immense force that often seems to surpass our innate boundaries, occasionally nudging us towards the brink of madness. Its capacity to inspire actions, evoke emotions, and propel individuals to extraordinary heights unveils the immense and unpredictable nature of this emotion. However, the lingering question remains: How does this enigmatic force either lead us astray towards self-destruction or elevate us to epitomize selflessness? It possesses the power to unravel both the magnificent and unforeseeable facets of human nature oscillating between good and evil. These unending inquiries paint a vivid canvas of the intricate and layered complexity of human relationships.

About The Author

Smriti Gupta, a debut author and an accomplished pharmaceutical professional, entrepreneur, and Executive Director of her startup, Vytis Pharmaceuticals, is deeply passionate about storytelling and exploring the intricacies of human emotions. Her academic journey boasts an illustrious path, marked by her alumni status at IIT(BHU), her distinction as a double gold medalist, and her dedicated research contributions that led to securing prestigious PhD scholarships at both Rovira i

Virgili University in Barcelona, Spain, and AIIMS, New Delhi. Her remarkable tenure as a DST INSPIRE research fellow under the Ministry of Science & Technology, Govt. of India, showcased her exceptional intelligence and expertise.

Raised in a small town, Smriti's fondness for literature ignited quite early in life, nurturing her fascination for crafting narratives that delve into the depths of human experiences. With a background in creative writing and a vivid imagination, her debut novel, *'Tangled Breaths of Love'*, is a testament to her commitment to creating captivating stories that resonate deeply with readers.

When not immersed in the world of words, Smriti finds joy in painting, dancing, savouring a good cup of coffee, and cherishing moments with her family. *'Tangled Breaths of Love'* marks her inaugural stride in a journey to share her distinct voice and narratives with the world.

www.ingramcontent.com/pod-product-compliance
Lightning Source LLC
LaVergne TN
LVHW091215150826
845672LV00005B/1374

* 9 7 9 8 8 9 2 3 3 8 2 9 5 *